To: ▮▮▮▮▮▮

From: Regina Herrera

Re: Junior Zombie Brigade

Importance level: HIGHEST

If you're reading this, it means you're part of the underground Junior Zombie Brigade. Thanks for all your help defending Redwood AND investigating ▮▮▮▮▮▮. But ▮▮▮▮▮▮ is on to us and will stop at nothing to protect their dangerous secrets.

I need your help more than ever. Are you ready to join the fight?

Scan this code to report for duty!

ZOMBIE SEASON

DEAD IN THE WATER

ZOMBIE SEASON

DEAD IN THE WATER

JUSTIN WEINBERGER

SCHOLASTIC PRESS / NEW YORK

FOR CHELSEA SHEA ENNEN, TO WHOM I SAY OBAH

Library of Congress Cataloging-in-Publication Data available

ISBN 978-1-338-88173-8

10 9 8 7 6 5 4 3 2 1   24 25 26 27 28

Printed in Italy   183

First edition, May 2024

Book design by Stephanie Yang

During the summer, the zombie horde kicks dust into the sky that doesn't settle for weeks.

The Dusk, people call it.

Even hundreds of miles away, it will tinge the whole horizon orange. At the peak of the season, the sun turns red, like the eye of some impossibly large monster. Peering at the world with boiling-hot fury.

But up in Alaska, on the Zarkovsky family's fishing boat, it's springtime and the night sky is so clear that you can see the famous aurora borealis—the northern lights. Unfortunately, it's not nighttime right now. It's the middle of the workday and the Zarkovskys are hauling in the daily catch. Business as usual.

"Let's get a move on, gang!" Alek Zarkovsky calls down to his four older brothers and four older cousins. They're on the deck of the boat, while twelve-year-old Alek and his three-day-younger cousin, Anton, stay up in the wheelhouse with the steering controls.

The older Zarkovskys roll their eyes and playfully accuse Alek of being afraid of getting his hands dirty. Alek would like nothing more than to help his family earn a living, but he and Anton are too young to do the heavy lifting. Instead, they watch and learn, and keep everything on the boat squeaky clean. Today, they've already finished that work, so they're staying out of the way and playing cards.

"Your turn, Alek," says Anton.

Alek peels a facedown card off the top of a pile in his hand, laying down a four of clubs.

Anton also plays a card without looking, and they both see it's a jack of diamonds. "Pick up the pace," Anton urges.

"I'm hurrying." Alek eagerly flings down a card from his stack. It's another jack.

Fast as they can, Alek and Anton both lunge forward and slap their hands down on the pile. Alek beats Anton by a fingernail with a cry of triumph. "Mine! Jack slap heeey!"

"Come on!" says Anton. "You didn't even lift your hand up off the card."

"Look. This is why no one else will play with you. You're a bad loser."

"But it's cheating. You have to lift your hand up and then slap it. You can't just—"

Alek lifts his hand. "Whatever, Anton. I don't care, take it."

Anton frowns, lifting his hand, too. "No. Fine, you take it."

The two jacks just sit there, staring back at them.

"This game will never end. Can't we call it a tie?"

"Pick up your cards, cheater," says Anton. "We're still playing."

Alek rolls his eyes and grins at his favorite cousin, his best friend. Alek is very accustomed to Anton's competitive nature. They're two of a kind. A pair of jacks, always together in whatever they do. For every class, they're seated next to each other. For every chore, they're a tag team. Over time they've naturally grown entangled, like two trees planted beside each other.

Suddenly, there's an alarmed commotion from outside:

"Whoa whoa whoa!"

Anton and Alek call time-out and head to the window that overlooks the deck below. Alek's uncle Pete—Anton's father—is using a crane to lift a net groaning with wriggling fish out of the water, hoisting it over the deck of the boat.

"Pete Pete Pete! Stop stop stop!" calls out Alek's oldest brother, Misha.

"Stop?" Uncle Pete calls back, over the sound of the motor. He pauses, leaving the heavy net hanging in midair.

"Stop! Get it off!" Misha shouts. "Throw it back!"

"Huh?!" Uncle Pete looks confused.

Alek follows Misha's eyeline and sees—

Something's wrong.

The net bulges and writhes.

A human-seeming arm pushes against the cords of rope, and Alek's gut drops. "No way," he says.

Uncle Pete doesn't see what Misha and Alek have.

He still looks confused: "What are you talking about?"

Misha rushes across the deck, taking control of the crane.

Only then does the truth become clear to everyone: The net that scooped up fish has harvested something else from the ocean floor as well. A sound emerges from the net—a howl of hunger. It makes Alek's blood go cold.

From the deep, they've hauled up a monster. A zombie.

And not just any zombie—it's huge. Giant-sized, fueled by all the fish in the net with it. It eats and eats as it hangs in midair. An enormous, cold-blooded monstrosity sucking all warmth from the air.

"Throw it back, before it's too late!" Alek's cousin Ozzie screams.

But as the crane moves closer to the sea, the net begins to split. A stream of fish spills out, pulling the tear wider as they tumble onto the deck.

Misha desperately works the controls of the crane.

"C'mon, c'mon—" Alek watches the net swing back and forth, the hole growing wider with each swing. If Misha can't maneuver the net over the water before the gash is big enough for the zombie to escape, the zombie will land right on the deck . . .

The net nears the side of the boat, then rips completely open. The zombie drops.

Misha cries out, a scream of fear . . . but it turns to a roar of victory as the zombie drops past the railing of the boat and disappears.

On the far side of the boat, there's a *splash!*

For a moment, everyone just stares. *Is it gone?*

Everything's silent.

Then the small noises return: The sound of fish trying to wriggle to the edge of the deck, back into the sea. The creak of the free-swinging fishing net. Uncle Pete's and Misha's uncomfortable chuckles at the close call. They grow and grow until everyone's laughing in relief, and in the wheelhouse, Alek grins widely at Anton. But then a tiny movement catches Alek's eye: A pencil rolls off the table and clatters to the floor.

Anton and Alek feel the ship tilt ever so slightly underfoot.

"Misha!" Alek calls, pointing to the lip of the boat. Two cold, dark eyes rise over the railing, staring hungrily.

The zombie.

It didn't plummet into the sea—it held on to the boat as it fell. And now it's climbing back up again.

Two giant hands grasp, pulling.

Bending the metal.

Lifting itself up.

As the zombie climbs, its weight makes the entire boat tip. The deck under the boys' feet slants more and more.

Anton loses his footing and starts to slide down. Gravity is pulling him hard.

He tumbles faster and faster, then slams against the wall of the cabin.

"Hold on!" Alek calls, helping Anton to his feet. "Life vests!"

Anton nods. "Got it!"

Grasping the wall for balance, Anton opens the cabinet containing emergency life vests and hands one to Alek. They each put one on, Alek's fingers fumbling with the clasp. Anton helps him fasten it.

Meanwhile, the boat continues to tilt toward the zombie as the Zarkovskys grab tight to keep from tumbling toward the slimy giant.

The zombie moans with a bottomless, greedy hunger. Everything not tied down slides toward the zombie's blue-veined, awful feet. Fish, ropes, coolers, Alek's brothers and cousins—

Alek can't see what happens next, because Anton pulls him to the ground.

"Stay down," Anton says with quiet force. "We need to get to the life raft."

"What?" says Alek. "But—"

"No buts. We're getting off this boat now." Anton crosses the cabin to the boat's controls and activates the emergency locator. It calls the coast guard automatically. Help will soon be on the way.

But it's too late to save the ship, Alek realizes when he lifts his eyes to take another glimpse out the window.

The zombie seems even bigger than before. As tall as the entire crane. The whole boat is tilted at an angle, fish and fishermen scrabbling with equal panic, trying to escape the giant's grasp.

Uncle Pete bursts into the wheelhouse, wild-eyed, with a forehead gash that's trickling blood into his eyes. "Uncle Pete?!" Alek shouts.

"Quiet, Alek," Uncle Pete hisses. He grabs both Alek and Anton by the shoulders and pulls them along with him. "Let's move. Now."

They turn to the door, moving as fast as they can while keeping quiet.

"What about Misha?" says Alek. "What about everyone else? We can't leave them behind!"

Before anyone can answer, there's a loud *bang* from over the side of the boat, and suddenly an emergency lifeboat starts to inflate into a kind of floating tent.

A series of splashes comes afterward—Alek's family jumping into the water—but he isn't sure if he hears eight of them.

"We're the last ones off the boat," Uncle Pete says. "You're gonna have to jump with me, okay?"

When Alek looks back toward the deck, just to make sure no one is left behind, he locks eyes with the towering zombie. Milky eyes rove around, not seeing the humans. In the lightless depths of the sea, vision isn't how it hunts.

Its nostrils flare as it catches the humans' scent.

A giant sticky hand reaches out, fumbling, searching, like a person grasping for popcorn in a dark movie theater.

Alek feels huge fingers wrap around his chest.

Squeezing him.

He tries to scream, but the only sound that comes out of him is a tiny huff of air.

He's about to be swallowed.

As Alek is lifted, caged in the giant's hand, he turns his head—

"Alek!"

Anton is coming back, reaching out—

Alek and Anton are pulled apart.

Squeezed, suffocating, lifted into the air, Alek watches Anton, even as Uncle Pete pulls Anton backward and throws him over the edge of the boat.

Splash.

Alek watches the icy water close over Anton's head. Then the life vest rockets him back up to the surface.

"Alek?!" Anton cries out.

Alek can't answer; he has no air left in his lungs.

"Alek!" Anton calls again and again.

But Alek's vision dwindles to a pinprick and goes dark.

1

STUXVILLE

Eleven-year-old Oliver Wachs and his nine-year-old sister, Kirby, stare at the all-you-can-eat breakfast buffet.

"I," says Kirby, "could get used to this."

"Dive in, kids," says Oliver's mom, handing them each a tray.

Oliver's dad ties an apron on over his clothes. "Go ahead and eat, you two. Mom and I are going to help serve food awhile."

After several weeks of eating emergency rations out of their go bags or sharing modest meals in zomb shelters, it's a treat for the Wachs family to see food like this.

Waffles so fresh you could find them by smell alone. Eggs in any possible form, including cheesy breakfast burritos wrapped up with crispy potatoes. Tangy orange juice you can squeeze yourself. Impossibly creamy yogurt, like ice cream but without the danger of a brain freeze. Unlimited hot chocolate in pre-warmed mugs . . .

"Is this what it feels like, being a zombie?" Oliver asks, staring hungrily at the smorgasbord.

"Maybe," says Kirby. "I always imagined it'd be like living in one of those online videos where everything is cake."

The idea of becoming a zombie makes Oliver shiver, like there's icing in his veins. He picks up a warm mug and fills it with hot chocolate, and for a moment he achieves perfect oneness with the universe. All his thoughts grow calm. He feels like he's floating inside the mug, hugged by giant hands. It's a nice change after everything he went through a few weeks ago: Getting caught in a huge Rogue Wave of zombies that decimated his hometown of Redwood. Encountering a new kind of foe that lurks in the water, immune to superchillers. Teaming up with his friend Regina to survive a surge of giant zombies and broadcast a message that warned the whole town . . .

This zombie season has been unlike anything Oliver has ever experienced, and it hasn't even peaked yet.

After piling their trays high with food, Oliver and Kirby search for a place to sit among all the other people in the large cafeteria-like space capable of feeding hundreds of hungry ZDPs. "ZDP" is an abbreviation for Zombie-Displaced Person, of course—folks like the Wachs family, and everyone else from Redwood, and everyone from towns *like* Redwood that've been evacuated. They're all taking shelter here in this building that's normally used as a college dorm, with communal bathrooms and little, tiny apartments with no kitchens or privacy anywhere.

After a string of overcrowded motels, Oliver is relieved to be in a place like this. And that relief multiplies as Oliver looks down a long row of tables and sees faces he recognizes.

People from Redwood, he realizes. Teachers from his school. Families from their neighborhood. Even this lady from the hardware store who always used to yell at him for touching the plants in the garden section when he was little.

At the sight of the familiar faces, Oliver feels a wave of homesickness.

Oliver is extremely eager to return to normal life. To be a regular kid again. To worry about balancing equations in math instead of multiplying zombies in the shadows. To ride his bike around town without always knowing his closest evacuation route. To eat one more slice of pizza at Cosmo's—even to have one more day at *school* . . .

Oliver feels a familiar wave of grief, and fights it off by thinking about the day when Redwood has finally been rebuilt exactly how it was—except this time totally zombieproof.

Lost in the daydream, his eyes wander and land on the woman from the hardware store.

"Our hero returns!" she says to Oliver as their eyes meet.

"Huh?" he says.

"Remarkable work, Ollie," says the man next to her. "Way to save the day."

Oliver awkwardly waves. He turns to Kirby. "Do we know him?"

"No idea," Kirby whispers. "Everyone's heard what you did, I guess."

"Come on. I didn't do *that* much."

"Getting that message out? Battling zombies, saving lives?"

"I was just doing what anyone would," Oliver insists, fighting to keep the embarrassment off his face.

He searches for a seat someplace out of the spotlight, and tries to ignore the eyes following him. The whispers making his ears prick up self-consciously. Oliver isn't *really* a hero. He's just as lucky to be alive as any other ZDP in Stuxville.

"Great stuff, Ollie! Can't wait to see what you pull off next!" says his old gym teacher, Mr. Stroman. It makes Oliver cringe to think about what's "next." They're not expecting him to, like, save the entire world, are they? Because Oliver doesn't have the first clue how to do that. He just wants to get back home again. To be a kid again, to draw his maps for fun and bother his aunt Carrie at work.

Amidst Oliver's distraction, he hears his name:

"Ollie Wachs!"

Oliver recognizes the voice instantly. The weight on his shoulders lifts as he turns to see his best friend, Del Shorter, standing up at a table.

Before Oliver can decide whether to hug his friend in excitement or just act cool, Kirby ditches her tray in Oliver's arms and rushes toward Del, going in for a hug.

The last day Oliver saw Del in person, Del was curled up in a ball on the floor of the Wachs family minivan. He'd gotten separated from his parents and was terrified that they'd been lost in the Rogue Wave.

Yet here he is smiling and laughing and eating with a bunch of kids

Oliver doesn't recognize. Is he okay now? Are his parents? Del's texts have all been really short, in both length and in details, so Oliver really doesn't know what's going on with his best friend.

Before Oliver has time to ask any questions, Del starts making rapid-fire introductions to everyone at the table. "This is the guy I told you about! He saved everyone in our neighborhood during the Rogue Wave. Everyone in the *city*, almost."

"It's no big deal," says Oliver, silently pleading with Del to stop.

"*You're* the guy Del keeps talking about, who made the maps?" says a slightly older kid with the build of a football player, who Del introduced as Milo. He shakes Oliver's hand and nearly crushes it with his strength. "Nice going, Wachs."

"Uh. Thanks, Milo."

"Did you really race the whole way to the zombie brigade head-quarters without shoes on?" asks a younger kid, eyes wide with wonder. Oliver doesn't even know how to answer that. Of course he was wearing shoes; how do people get these ideas?

"*I* think you just got really lucky," says a weedy boy, Conrad.

Oliver feels himself shrink away from Conrad, as this accusation echoes Oliver's own silent fear: Oliver *did* get really lucky.

"You weren't there, Conrad," Kirby pipes up, bristling.

She defends her brother, telling everyone all about Oliver's bravery and resourcefulness as he made the dangerous trek through mudslides and the ruins of the town. How he snuck past a zombie giant in order to alert everyone before it was too late. But even as Oliver listens to her, he has this sinking feeling:

What if Conrad's right?

Deep down, Oliver is pretty sure that he's not the person they expect him to be. He's just like everyone else, nothing special. But now apparently people expect him to repeat his heroics. To do it again.

Oliver eats his breakfast quietly, deflecting attempts to make him talk about what happened in Redwood. And as the conversation moves on, Oliver silently thinks about Regina Herrera . . .

Regina, who is the *real* hero of Redwood. Who recruited Oliver to help her save the city. Who figured out how to get past the zombies between them and their goal. Who actually saved Oliver's life by risking her own to come back for him when he fell behind.

If not for her, Oliver wouldn't even be alive right now.

Ever since they parted ways, she's been texting him about "something new" she's working on, "something big." More than once, she's asked him if he wants to help her. But Oliver keeps coming up with excuses.

She's not taking Oliver's no for an answer, though. She keeps asking "Why not?" . . . just keeps pushing and pushing. He's running out of ways to say no that aren't the truth, which is: "I'm afraid of letting you down."

He's ashamed of this. To be afraid, despite all the cheers he just received? Seriously? It makes Oliver feel like a jerk. Doubly so since it's Regina—who saved his life—who needs *him*.

And so, before he gets distracted again, Oliver summons the nerve to take out his phone and text Regina. Despite his fears and doubts, he has to *try*.

Hey, he writes. *Do you still need any help?*

The moment he hits send, he jumps at the sound of two screeching girls rushing toward him and the other ZDP kids.

"Ollie!" Chanda Cortez plunks down her tray, squeezing in on the bench, which is way too crowded already.

"Kirby!" says Chanda's best friend Darlene Reiner, joining the group as well.

"Del!" they both say simultaneously.

As Del introduces Chanda and Darlene to the whole group of his new friends, Kirby nudges Oliver.

"It's a Redwood reunion!" says Kirby.

"Maybe we're finally getting back to normal," Oliver suggests, hopeful as he can be.

"This is just the beginning," Kirby reminds him. "One foot in front of the other, right?"

"What?" he asks her. The words are familiar, but it doesn't sound like something Kirby would say.

"That's what your notebook said on the cover, isn't it?"

His beloved green notebook, filled with detailed maps and notes he made of all the secret things he discovered exploring his hometown.

"It totally did," Oliver says, surprised that he could've forgotten the words on the notebook he looked at every day. The notebook that helped

15

Oliver and his family escape a zombie wave . . . but the notebook itself didn't fare as well. It's now blotchy with faded ink and caked with mud, and every time he opens it another page crumbles to dust. It's in a Ziploc bag in his suitcase. He can't bear to touch it for fear of it falling apart completely.

But his sister's right.

He reaches into his back pocket, taking out a new green notebook. It's blank and empty, because he hasn't been in one place long enough to start exploring and recording his findings in it.

But this moment feels right to start again. Here, at breakfast, surrounded by friends from Redwood, he feels a little more alive, finally. He uncaps a marker and inks on the cover *One Foot in Front of the Other.*

"That's more like it," says Oliver.

"It's a fresh start," says Kirby with a grin. But just as he starts to feel like maybe things are truly going in the right direction, Del has a surprise for Oliver.

"Ready, Ollie?" says Del.

"For what?"

Suddenly, Del's new friends all rise in a group.

Del stands, too, with a gleam in his eye. "Manhunt!"

"Manhunt?" says Oliver.

"Yeah," says Del. "You remember . . . that game we've played our whole lives, to train for escaping the zombies? One kid's a 'human' and the rest of us are 'zombies' chasing them?"

Del grins at his joke. They both know that Oliver isn't confused about what the game is. What Oliver finds surprising is that they're playing it at the height of actual zombie season.

"Come on, we can't be late—these guys take it very seriously. Like you always wanted Coach to do, remember?" Del says as Milo and Conrad and Del's other new friends take their unfinished food and dump it in the trash. Oliver frowns at this, and stays planted in front of his meal.

"Come on, Del!" Milo calls. "Zombies don't take breaks and neither do we!"

"Aye aye, Captain," says Del. "You coming, Ollie?"

He and the others head toward the doors leading to the perfectly mowed grass in the center of the Stuxville University campus.

"Can't we just hang out? I haven't seen you in weeks."

"Ollie, we can hang out whenever," says Del. "This is important."

Oliver hesitates, stung by Del's clear desire to be with his new friends.

"You *really* want to play Manhunt?" Oliver asks. "You were never that interested back home."

"That's the whole problem, Ollie," says Del. "You of all people remember how much of a loser I was in Redwood. How I was too scared to stand up for my friends. My family. That can't happen next time. I gotta practice as much as I can."

"You're not a loser, Del," says Oliver.

Del looks upset for a moment, but then he nods. "That's right," he says. "Not anymore."

"You're a good guy, Del. When we get you back to Redwood—"

"*If* we get back to Redwood, you mean."

Oliver feels the ground under his feet shift. Or it's his legs that get a little wobbly, maybe. "What do you mean, *if* we get home?"

Del blinks. "Ollie. Come on. You don't seriously think we'll just go back to the way things were, do you? Our houses are gone. Half of Redwood is wreckage. Plus, there are zombies in the water now? And that's not mentioning any of the other towns that need help even more than Redwood. Like where the other guys are from."

Oliver looks at Del, seeing how serious he is. How certain. "And also? I don't really *want* things to go back to the way they were, Ollie."

With that, Del heads outside, leaving it up to Oliver whether to join him or not.

Oliver's phone buzzes. It's a photo from Regina—a picture from a hilltop overlooking Redwood. It's littered with wrecked buildings and washed-out roads. There are still husks of extinguished zombies on the ground.

Greetings from Redwood, another text follows. *Wish you were here.*

Before he can respond, a third text appears.

I need your help more than ever.

His phone rings.

It's Regina.

2

WORK IN PROGRESS

Deep in the dark, zombie-ravaged husk of the HumaniTeam office in Redwood, California, Regina Herrera sits in front of a glowing computer screen.

Through the earbud that's connected to her cell phone, she hears a voice. It's Oliver Wachs.

"Regina? Hello? Are you there?"

"Hey," Regina says into the earbud. "About time you called."

"I didn't call. You did."

"Because you finally texted me back!" says Regina, annoyed. "Are you avoiding me?"

"No," Oliver says, too quickly. "I just . . . I'm just super busy trying to survive zombie season. Like all the rest of us ZDPs."

Regina bites back a snarky reply. About how busy *she's* been, trying to make sure zombie season doesn't become totally *impossible* to survive. A project she sure could've used more help with. But Joule's gone to New York, and Oliver's been reluctant to lend a hand. It's only the Junior Zombie Brigade who allowed Regina to get this far. And now her family friend named Kai is helping, too. A boy her age whose dad is even more important at HumaniTeam than Regina's parents.

Regina doesn't tell Oliver any of that, though.

"I'm glad we're talking now, Ollie."

"Me too," Oliver agrees.

Regina remembers standing with Oliver on the hilltop overlooking their ruined hometown, surveying the damage of the zombie wave they barely survived.

She will never forget how her whole body buzzed with exhaustion.

How she felt completely emptied out and filled up at the same time.

Alive. That's how she felt. Connected to all the people gathered on other hilltops surrounding Redwood. People who were safe because of what Regina accomplished. With Oliver's help, of course. She'll never forget the race to zombie brigade HQ, broadcasting the emergency message that warned everyone to get to high ground—leading a group of surging amphibious zombies on a chase that no one but Regina Herrera and Oliver Wachs could've pulled off . . . It was incredible.

And yet, things are worse than ever now.

First, her parents didn't seem to care how many people she had saved. "I only care about one life, Gina, and that's yours," her father said, furious with her for taking on such a terrible risk. "We're going to supervise you much more closely now," he announced, and followed through by taking a leave of absence from his job to homeschool her in their new rental apartment in Berkeley.

Second, Regina has learned that a growing number of zombies are becoming immune to superchillers—the world's main zombiefighting tool. The supercooled water makes them *stronger*, in fact. Even worse? HumaniTeam—the company responsible for inventing the superchiller— knows all about it. But they're hiding it from the world.

Regina's mother uncovered this truth during the Rogue Wave, and she's been shouting her discovery to the world, even though it meant losing her job. But it's been weeks now, and HumaniTeam has attacked Dr. Herrera's reputation relentlessly. As a result, the world is unwilling to believe the warning she is giving them.

Which is why Regina is here. She needs to find some way to convince the world that HumaniTeam are the bad guys. To expose the truth and stop them before they can cause more damage.

But before Regina can do any of that, she needs *proof* that they have been lying about everything.

Her parents can never know what she's *really* up to, of course.

Not until she's gotten what she came for.

Then she'll tell them everything, and they'll hold a big press conference and the world will turn against HumaniTeam, for creating zombies that are basically invincible.

And when *Regina* unveils *her* secret research, it will be even more explosive than the truth that her mother uncovered. She has a lead on a super secret project that's even more dangerous to HumaniTeam. *Project Phoenix*.

"You still there, Regina?" says Oliver. "I don't have much time . . ."

"Well, Ollie," she says, "neither does the world."

"I hear you, Regina. I'm trying to help."

Regina sighs. "You really want to help, Ollie?" she says, nervous about the answer. But Oliver doesn't hesitate.

"I'll do my best," he says, sounding nervous as well.

"Can you come up with some excuse to get your aunt to bring you to Redwood? You could say you want to help with the cleanup."

"I'd *love* to help with the cleanup. I really want to come home again. Just . . . have everything back to normal, you know?"

"Yes!" says Regina. "That's perfect, say it just like that. But that's only our cover story."

She explains how her brilliant mother, who quit HumaniTeam after discovering their dangerous lies, needs a smoking gun. Proof of HumaniTeam's crimes.

"Whoa, back up," Oliver demands. "Crimes?"

"Oliver, I don't have time to explain everything. I need you to trust me, okay?"

"I trust you," he says, though he doesn't sound happy about it.

"You have to listen, Ollie—that giant zombie we saw in Redwood? It was created by HumaniTeam. By the Cloudbusters and superchillers we use all the time. All the energy it takes to create supercooled water, it's making zombies even more dangerous. Causing some of them to transform. To become immune to water entirely."

"Like at the brigade headquarters?" Oliver asks. They both remember what they saw that day during Oliver's heroic race to warn the population to get to safety.

"Exactly! The water tower, remember?"

Regina recalls the zombies throwing themselves against the walls of the Redwood Zombie Brigade Headquarters. How they were battering themselves senseless to try and topple the tower full of supercooled water on the roof. And eventually, when they succeeded?

When supercooled water is used on one of these amphibious zombies, it actually *supercharges* them. It makes them become *giants*.

To make matters worse—so, so much worse!—HumaniTeam just successfully tested a new technology that's even *more* powerful than a superchiller. A Cloudbuster rocket, which can summon a powerful thunderstorm that destroys an entire horde.

It's like a million superchillers all at once.

Everyone thinks that it's going to allow humans to live normal lives again.

But there's one problem . . . A rocket with the power of a million superchillers also speeds up the zombies' resistance. Creating giant amphibious zombies a million times faster.

Regina's mother has been pleading with everyone far and wide to listen before it's too late: Stop using Cloudbusters.

But HumaniTeam has done everything in its enormous power to make sure people don't listen to her. To protect their business, not the planet.

"Regina," says Oliver, "what are we going to do?"

"We're going to show the world that HumaniTeam can't be trusted. That when they say Cloudbusters will bring an end to zombie season . . . it's only true if you realize that they're not going to get rid of zombies, they're just going to make it so they're here all year round. Unless we do something right now, before the damage is done, zombie season will never end."

"Wow," says Oliver. "And . . . and you have proof?"

"I will soon," says Regina.

"Soon?"

"I'm looking, Ollie! I know the files exist. What they did to Nix. During Project Phoenix . . ."

"What's Nix? And Project what?"

"I'll tell you everything later. But right now, what I need from you is a map."

"A map?"

"The zombies came into Redwood through tunnels, remember? And the tunnels are still here. It's how I've been sneaking in and out of this building—but this is taking a lot longer than I thought. And I can't keep using the one passage I know about, or I'll get caught. If I'm onto the truth and they find out? They're willing to let the world end rather than lose their profits. What wouldn't they do to silence me? So. I need to stay ahead. I need a map of the whole zombie subway system. And that's a job for Ollie Wachs."

3

BELLY OF THE BEAST

On a New York City beach, there are many strange sights, Joule Artis has discovered. But as she gazes out into the water—only a ferry ride from her new apartment—what she sees there is from another world.

At first, she can't quite make it out, so she moves closer.

"Joule, stay with me!" her mother says sharply.

Joule slows down, but doesn't stop.

Surfers are gathered around something in the water. Something big. But she still can't tell what it is, and her curiosity pulls her in even closer. As the waves push and push, she spots the huge dorsal fin, the massive tail, the wide mouth full of sharp teeth.

"Mom, it's a *whale*," says Joule with a sharp inhale.

The surfers are trying to help it.

"We need a rope!" the surfers plead as everyone up and down the beach races toward the commotion.

"Rope!" Joule adds her voice to the pleas. She feels her heart pump hard as she imagines the animal's pain.

It's as big as a bus, but far from fully grown. It shouldn't be suffering like this . . . It shouldn't be alone like this. Joule instantly thinks of her father, who dedicated his life to helping animals like this one. He isn't here to help anymore, though. He died last summer in an unnatural disaster that was too small to be named or remembered.

It's only very recently that Joule has finally accepted the truth—that her father is really gone. Somehow that has made everything even harder than before for Joule.

What would Dad do? Joule asks herself. But there's no clear way to help.

"You can do it!" Joule calls out with all her heart. To the surfers, to the whale, to the entire planet. Still, the tide is working against them. Soon the animal will be fully up on the sand, unless humans can help it.

"I'm calling for help," someone says.

"Tell them it's still alive," Joule replies. Joule turns and sees it's her mother making the call. She feels herself dare to hope as she sees the creature's mouth open and close slightly. The whale's movements are weak as the waves push it and pull it in the surf. But it seems to be alive.

"Rope!" calls out a lifeguard, dashing up the beach and diving in the water, carrying a loop of rope.

Then Joule sees something that freezes her blood.

She looks closer as the jaw opens and closes.

In the darkness of the whale's mouth, there's a gentle glow. And a soft sound emerges, too. A gurgle, sort of. A wet sigh, almost.

It's a moan, she realizes with a shudder.

Joule feels her throat tighten in fear as understanding floods her mind.

"Get back, get back!!" Joule screeches to the people trying to help the whale. The people who haven't had to spend quite so much of their lives in constant terror, so they're not ready for what's about to happen here.

This is a zombie attack.

The whale is like a Trojan horse.

"Run! RUN! Get to high ground now!" Joule calls to the rescuers, then adds to her mother, "It's like the ones in Redwood, Mom. The ones that—that—"

Joule knows that her mother remembers the giant amphibious zombie that nearly tore her life away just weeks ago, back in California. Before they came to New York to be safe from such threats.

The people in the water turn to face her in confusion. They don't see the whale's mouth open wider and wider behind them, while the body moves unnaturally. Like something is emerging from a cocoon. As if the body is a husk, and something inside is fighting to get out.

Joule watches, horrified. A swollen, squelching giant zombie muscles up the dying whale's throat, into its mouth. It looks out at the surfers, who are all facing Joule.

Slime covers the zombie's translucent skin, and its jaw hangs open. The muscles are too strong to ever fully close, except when it makes a powerful, bone-snapping bite. And even having fed so recently on such a huge animal from the inside out, its need for *more* has grown to match the size of its fourteen-foot-tall frame.

It reaches for one of the surfers with a hand that tears through their wet suit and into the skin underneath.

And then the monster and its human prey disappear underwater, leaving no sign of their existence behind.

Swept away. Out of sight.

Gone without a struggle.

One by one, the other surfers are pulled under the water and do not reappear. Everyone on the beach and in the water screams.

"Out of the water!" the lifeguard bellows, blasting a whistle again and again. It's too late now, though. Much too late.

4

ZDPS

"He's over here!" Conrad calls, leaping out of a hiding place right next to Oliver.

"Huh?" says Oliver, startled. He stumbles and trips, ending up on his back in the dirt.

Conrad laughs. He strides over to Oliver, looming over him with a toothy smile. Appearing every bit as dangerous as the zombie he's imitating. "That all you got, hero?"

Slowly, Conrad reaches down and taps Oliver on the forehead, right between the eyes.

"You're dead, Ollie."

Oliver just lies there, blinking.

Manhunt is a traditional game in zombie-infested areas, where there's one "human" player whose job is to avoid capture by the others—the "zombie horde"—as long as possible. It's fun to play, except that the zombies almost always win sooner or later. In fact, back in Redwood, Oliver was one of the only kids in his neighborhood who could "survive" long enough for the "zombies" to give up on finding him.

But here at the ZDP center, it's much more competitive.

For Del and his new friends, it's not a game. It's serious. It's *training*. They're totally focused on becoming elite zombiefighters once they're old enough, and this is how they're practicing. Even though they're all way too young to even be cadets, of course.

"Conrad's up next!" Milo calls out as he jogs up and helps Oliver to his feet. "Walk it off, Wachs."

"You'll do better tomorrow," says Del supportively.

In truth, Oliver is hardly concentrating on the game. His conversation with Regina has been stuck in his head on a loop. That HumaniTeam's zombiefighting tools—both the weather-altering Cloudbusters and the traditional superchillers—are only solving the zombie problem on the *surface*, while making the *underlying* problems worse and worse. Transforming the zombies themselves . . . ?

He's got to get to Redwood, both to help Regina and to see her proof with his own eyes.

But the next day he's even more distracted and frustrated and he finds himself flat on his back again, for the second time. Caught by Conrad even faster than before. "Pitiful," says Conrad, with no mercy.

As Oliver catches his breath, his phone buzzes.

Status report? Regina texts him. *Stop messing around, Ollie.*

Oliver burns with irritation as Del helps him to his feet. He's doing his best to get there. But it's not easy to figure out how. His aunt has a big job to do, and his parents have their hands full with figuring out how the family is going to get back on its feet.

So here he is, stuck playing Manhunt, day after day, as the texts from Regina get more and more urgent:

Can I count on you or not? Regina texts, as the week goes on.

And Oliver is starting to wonder that, too. It feels like he's definitely going to let her down. Distracted by this, he's no match for the ZDP kids in Stuxville.

"Come on, Ollie!" Del complains as he tags Oliver. "You're not even trying."

"I've got nothing to prove to these guys, Del," says Oliver.

"Well, I do," says Del. "And I need you to help me get better."

"Why?" asks Oliver.

"You *know* why," says Del quietly. "When the zombies showed up last time, you saved the entire town. But what did I do? I crumbled, Ollie. And next time it happens? It can't be like before. I have to be strong. To fight."

Del is so ashamed of not being "heroic like Oliver" that he's pushing himself *way* too hard. It's the thing that upsets Oliver most about these games of Manhunt. Even though it's clear that Del's improving . . . it's *also* clearly doing more harm than it could possibly do good.

Like scratching open a wound so it heals badly. So it's always stinging and bleeding, and turning into a scar.

It's turning Del into something he's not. It's twisting him.

There are important things that Del does so naturally—being a good friend, being curious about the world, being thoughtful and generous. Just being around him has made Oliver a better person, too.

But all Del values now is the skill to survive zombies. That's the only measure of himself he cares about.

So it's up to Oliver to show up for his friend, he decides. To be a reminder of everything Del has forgotten he's so good at. A reflection of Del himself.

But he also *really* has to find a way to get to Redwood. And so, on day four, when the game of Manhunt ends in a draw, he's thrilled to see a *perfect* opportunity arrive:

"Time out!" shouts Milo. "Brigadier sighting!"

Heads swivel instantly. Everyone sees what Milo noticed: An official zombie brigade cruiser pulls up and parks by the dorm.

A car that's armored against zombie attack, and carrying a fifty-gallon tank of supercooled water, to supply an entire squad of brigadiers' C-packs. From the driver's seat, a woman in a long zombieproof jacket emerges.

"Aunt C?" calls out Oliver in excitement. It's his aunt Carrie—known to everyone else as Chief Carrie Wachs, former leader of the Redwood Zombie Brigade and current leader of the state advanced tactics division. A few other ZDP kids rush over to her to ask about missing relatives and friends, to see if there still might be survivors out there.

She's speaking too quietly for Oliver to overhear the exact words, but it doesn't sound very hopeful. She's taking time to talk to each kid with patience and compassion, though. It makes Oliver grateful that she's his aunt.

"Hey, Ollie?" Del nudges him.

"Hey."

"Do you think your aunt would let us fight with her this summer?"

Oliver blinks. "What?"

"Like, let us join the brigade, even though we're too young."

"Oh," says Oliver. "I'm . . . not sure . . ."

"She's working out in the field, right? Search and rescue?"

"I think she's working on new strategies to fight the zombies these days. How to deal with a surge from the sea. How to evacuate people faster, smarter."

"That sounds like something I could do."

"Del . . . maybe you should give yourself a break and be a kid."

"No. That's the last thing I need," Del replies. "What I need is to get ready to fight next time. Like you."

"You don't need to soak a million zombies to be part of the fight, Del."

Del's expression starts to get cloudy, frustrated. "Ollie . . ."

But then Del stiffens, like a soldier during inspection. Oliver turns and follows his gaze, seeing Chief Wachs walk toward them just as Kirby arrives, too.

"I missed you guys," she says as Kirby releases her from a hug.

"Maybe you should come live with us, Aunt C," Kirby suggests hopefully.

"I won't be gone this long next time, Kirby, I promise," says Chief Wachs. "I've just been working hard."

Then she looks at Oliver and smiles. "What's it like to be a hero?"

Oliver looks away in embarrassment. But she hugs him and says, "Wanna see something I've been working on?"

"Sure," says Oliver.

"I've been dying to show you our newest project. Give me your phone," says Chief Wachs.

Oliver hands it over, and she downloads something on it.

"This is still in testing. For official use only," says Chief Wachs. "But I think you deserve to see what you've inspired with your clever little maps."

As Oliver takes his phone, he sees there's a new icon on the screen. An app labeled *Mapmaker Alpha*. "What's this?" Oliver asks as he opens it and sees the outlines of a map of Stuxville.

"You don't recognize it?" says Chief Wachs. "It's modeled off that notebook in your pocket, after all."

"What do you mean?" asks Oliver, still puzzled.

"We built a tool so our brigadiers—and dedicated explorers like you— can help create a new, constantly updating map of what's really out there in the world," explains Chief Wachs. "That way, if the roads aren't useful during the next crisis, *anyone* can use this to find a path to safety—like you used your notebooks and maps."

"Really?" Oliver feels a surge of pride.

As he experiments, he realizes the program is like a natural extension of his notebook in the virtual world. And other people have already sketched out new discoveries on it—details about the natural and built environment. Oliver feels himself almost vibrating with nervous energy. It's like he's scared—but not in a bad way. "This is really all because of my notebook?"

"All I did was take what you did and adapt it," his aunt says. "Without you, I would never have thought to make something like this, Oliver. I'm really, really proud of you, okay?"

Oliver blushes and nods. He's flustered and full of questions, but he remembers Regina, toiling away in Redwood, and summons all his willpower.

"Hey, Aunt C?" he asks. "Can I ask you a favor?"

"Yes, Ollie?"

"So, Regina Herrera told me that they need help with the cleanup in Redwood—"

Chief Wachs cuts him off. "Ollie, I know you really want to get back there. It's not time yet. Okay?"

"Aunt C . . . ?"

"I'm very busy right now, Ollie."

Oliver is about to plead more, but Del beats him to it. "It's not *just* Ollie who wants to help, Chief," he announces. "I'm ready to go, too. So are a lot of other kids around here. We can do anything you need. We *will* do anything you need. Let us help. You won't regret it."

Chief Wachs looks from Del to Oliver to the other ZDP kids nearby, all of them nodding in response to Del's urging.

Chief Wachs frowns.

"Please, Aunt C?" Oliver asks.

"*Any* job?" says Chief Wachs.

"Any job," Del agrees.

"Even one where we just clean up trash . . . ?"

"If that's what we have to do to prove ourselves," says Del.

"Well. If you can get a whole work group together to clean up Redwood, how could I say no to chaperoning the zombiefighters of the future on a trip to clean up their home?"

By the end of Chief Wachs's visit that night, it's all settled. With the support of Del and the other ZDPs, Oliver's aunt agrees to supervise them for a trip to Redwood in three days.

When Oliver texts Regina the good news, she texts back, *Can't you get here sooner?*

Classic Regina.

I'll see you in three days, Oliver writes back to her.

5

NRG

Regina Herrera has learned more about zombies in the last few weeks than she had in her previous twelve years of being on the planet.

Each time she sneaks into the abandoned HumaniTeam office, she learns more and more.

She's learned that there've been flashpoints for much longer than anyone ever told her, for one thing. Going back decades. Long before the summer sky turned Dusk orange.

She's learned that the amphibious zombies that she and Oliver faced off against in Redwood have been gathering in dead zones at the bottom of the sea, too.

The biggest thing Regina has discovered? She has so much more to learn.

She taps her fingers on the desk, disturbing the dust that's been gathering ever since the facility shut down after the disaster that ruined her family name. It was once almost a second home to her, and her familiarity with the place is why she is able to unearth the secrets hidden here. But the zombies damaged the building's power, limiting her access to just the files on drives she can connect to a laptop running on battery. Only after she recruited her wily family friend Kai Stone to help did the servers in a different part of the building somehow get power. It gave Regina access to new giant archives to comb through. And at long last, she's finally found something that starts her heart racing.

Firebird, she sees on the screen.

"Firebird" is another name for "phoenix."

And Project Phoenix is the name of HumaniTeam's secret zombie experiment that somehow unlocked zombie intelligence.

"They have a code name *for their code name*," Regina complains as she clicks open the file.

"You talking to me?" asks Kai.

Regina looks over, smiling. "Come look. Whatever you did to get this stuff working, Kai? It's worth it."

"Dark magic, pacts with the devil, that sort of thing," says Kai with a lopsided smile as he approaches.

She and Kai are both clever and ambitious. They're a natural team. And yet, Regina has been hesitant to trust him completely. She knows how selfish he can be. Always looking out for himself. But he is also cocky enough to spy on HumaniTeam without giving it a second thought.

On the screen, the file hasn't opened as it should.

"Hold on," says Regina. "Something went wrong."

She clicks again. The file won't open.

File corrupt, the computer tells her.

"No," says Regina. "No no no."

No matter how many times she tries to open the file, she gets the same response.

The proof she needs is close enough to touch, and yet . . .

"How could it be corrupted?" she asks, furious.

Kai peers over her shoulder. "Well, maybe because that file is older than we are, for one thing."

Regina looks at the date the file was created. It's nearly twenty years old, she realizes.

"What *is* Project Phoenix, anyway?" asks Kai.

"You wouldn't believe me," she says, not quite sure whether to tell Kai everything she knows about HumaniTeam's secret zombie experiments.

But before she can do anything else, the computer just goes black and shuts down.

"Hey!" says Regina. "What did you do?"

"I didn't touch a thing!"

As they look at each other, all the other computers go out, too.

"Kai? What's going on?"

"Regina?" Kai's voice reverberates in the darkness of the abandoned HumaniTeam office. It would've been loud enough to wake the dead, if any of them were still hibernating in the middle of the summer, at the peak of zombie season.

"What did you do, Kai?" Regina whispers, grabbing a flashlight, moving the beam side to side, scanning the pitch-dark room, peering out into the hallway.

Empty, as it should be.

No signs of zombies. Or worse, humans.

If zombies show up, all Regina and Kai have to worry about is life and death—but if they're spotted here by humans? That'd be a true nightmare. All those awkward questions about the research she's doing out here would come first, followed by Regina getting grounded for life. So Regina keeps her eyes wide open and her ears pricked.

She still jumps a little as Kai's pale face and red hair appear in the beam of her flashlight.

"Power went out," says Kai. "You head back and cover for me. I'll check out what happened."

"We're not splitting up," says Regina.

"It's perfectly safe," says Kai. "Really."

From Kai's insistence, Regina gets the sense that he doesn't want her to follow him. But this only makes Regina more curious, of course.

Though she knows it's time to get back to her father, something tells her she needs to see whatever Kai's doing, too. He's smart and gets things done, but he's also kind of sneaky and definitely needs to be watched.

"I'm coming with you, Kai. Lead the way."

"If you insist," he says, sounding slightly irritated.

Kai leads her left, right, down a stairwell. Regina knows these corridors and offices like she knows the layout of her own home. She spent many hours here with her parents in the years they worked here. In her memory, she sees it as it used to be: full of activity, with passionate, hardworking people coming and going at all hours of the day and night.

Those days are gone now. The Naturally Regenerating Generator that they created, which was supposed to transform the energy of zombies' movement into electricity to power the planet, went all wrong. The generator had actually been Regina's idea, and she'd felt responsible for the ruin of her family, and for the Rogue Wave that followed . . . but it's more complicated than that. Only one thing is very, very clear to Regina: HumaniTeam is willing to take enormous risks, but if something goes wrong, they always have someone else to blame. It's never their fault, according to them.

Regina intends to punish them for all their crimes. For the good of humanity.

"Kai?" she says. "Where are we going?"

Regina plays her flashlight over the passageway, following a long line of scars on the wall—like five claws scraping.

"Basement. Don't freak out," Kai tells Regina as he closes the basement door behind them. It booms as it strikes the doorjamb hard. Echoing all around—and ringing in Regina's head.

Ahead, there's a moaning sound.

Regina freezes in place.

"Everything's fine, okay?" says Kai. "I've got it covered."

She shines her flashlight ahead—

Gemlike orange eyes dazzle in the darkness, glassy and lifeless—all of them staring right at Regina.

Under those eyes, a snakelike, unhinged jaw hangs open. Her eyes move down. Arms dangling, hands twitching. Fingernails caked with dark material . . . dirt, or something worse. Their wordless, greedy moans are filled with a bottomless need. A hunger that only grows and grows.

Zombies.

The ringing in Regina's ears continues, louder.

"Kai, what is happening?"

"Relax, Regina," Kai says. "Like I said, it's under control. It's *perfectly* safe. Just out of fuel," he continues, stepping back outside the basement door, leaving Regina alone with the zombies.

"Kai!!"

"Be right back! Don't worry!"

Before Regina can fully process that she's alone in a room full of zombies, Kai rushes back in with two huge bags of trash.

He moves through the basement, weaving around the zombies. The creatures are all inside a chain-link fence, Regina sees. A cage.

The zombies can barely lift their arms in their weak, starved state. Stumbling too slowly to catch a snail.

Something about this whole arrangement strikes Regina as familiar.

Then, abruptly, she has a flash of a memory. A mine shaft full of zombies, turned into a generator. Project Coloma.

Shining her flashlight around the basement, she sees there's a complicated-looking treadmill on the ground, and it connects to a series of gears—a turbine. Regina understands what this is.

"Kai. You *didn't*," she says, a complicated mixture of feelings rising up inside her. Anger, helplessness, resolve. Exhaustion and determination. Regret. This is the prototype of what became the NRG—the Naturally Regenerating Generator. Kai has rebuilt it from machinery in storage here in the basement.

"This can't be happening again," Regina says.

The whole reason she's in here doing this work is to *stop* experiments like this—to stop HumaniTeam from making the zombie problem worse and worse—

Kai opens the trash bags and dumps the contents—a load of compost like corncobs and chicken bones—into a machine. As she watches, a banana peel falls onto the ground at the base of the machine. The zombies all turn, looking at it. Shambling toward it. As they do, the treadmill starts to turn.

A light bulb begins to shine—brown, then yellow, then white.

Zombie-powered.

Kai shrinks slightly under her judgmental glare. "Don't look at me like that. It's totally safe."

"It's *impossible* to make the NRG totally safe," Regina snaps. "My parents already learned that the hard way."

"Well, you and I won't make the same mistake this time."

"You are exactly like your dad," Regina says.

"Thank you," Kai says, smiling.

"That wasn't a compliment, Kai. I meant that you're reckless. You could start another flashpoint! I'm not a part of this. You knew I wouldn't be okay with this! That's why you didn't want me to come down and see what you did."

"Look. You said that you needed access to the old servers to do your research, and I got you access. You've been using good, clean, undetectable zombie power for days. All that time you didn't ask any questions about how I got the job done. You didn't care."

"I shouldn't have ever brought you here," Regina says. "Trusting you was a mistake."

"Regina. It's working! Problem solved! What's gotten into you these days?"

"This isn't about me, Kai," Regina tells him.

But it is about her, a little bit.

Okay, more than a bit.

Okay, it's *all* about Regina.

It's about how hard it was for Regina to make new habits and trust people. It's about an unsettling experience she had with the zombie who called himself Nix, who revealed things about Regina she's not sure she's ready to accept. It's about all the things she struggled with and barely survived during the Rogue Wave. She's not the same person Kai remembers. She's learned from some of her mistakes—mistakes that Kai reminds her about with his every comment and choice.

She's furious as she marches back upstairs. She's not going to be part of another disaster.

Regina and Kai head back to the place where the zombies' tunnel yawns open, and move in angry silence through the claustrophobic cavern and back out into the afternoon sun and sweltering heat. Robotically, Regina covers up the entrance, so it's harder to see, and then puts on an expression like everything's normal.

In moments, she's once more surrounded by workers rebuilding the town of Redwood. A sea of cranes and backhoes, cement mixers and pickup trucks.

But for Regina, the rot feels like it might be too deep to fix.

———

Meanwhile, in the basement of the HumaniTeam regional offices, behind a chain-link fence, one of the zombies trudging along the treadmill finds a surprising new reservoir of energy.

The zombie looks out, staring at the door where Regina Herrera stood moments before. *She's alive*, he thinks, with something a little bit like pride.

The zombie keeps walking, step after impossible step.

It shouldn't be possible for a zombie to think through a problem like this. Zombies aren't supposed to be intelligent.

But this specific zombie has been extensively prodded by clever, curious, cruel scientists who wanted to see if zombies could be rehabilitated into productive members of society. Though the project was buried deep and left forgotten, there were certain results.

And deep in the back of this zombie's starved mind, something's been reawakened. A need that's even deeper than the need for fuel that animates all the others trapped here.

This zombie's deepest hunger is to not be alone.

Come back, the zombie tries to call out to Regina Herrera. *It's me. It's Nix.*

But in Nix's infinite exhaustion, all that emerges is an unintelligibly faint sigh.

And soon he sinks back into a hibernation-like state—

Until he hears a sound once more . . .

Footsteps, coming back down the stairs.

The basement door opening, and a human silhouette standing framed in it.

Shining a light at the zombies, the human moves toward the trapped creatures behind the fence. Examining their faces.

It's her, Nix sees. Regina.

Here! he tries to say. *I'm here.*

Nix moves toward her with the last of his strength, and the flashlight lands on his face.

"*Nix?*" she whispers, perfectly shocked.

6

ANTON

This isn't real, Anton reminds himself, every night.

When Anton closes his eyes to sleep, it feels like floating in an endless ocean. Waves rising and falling. Icy water numbing his legs. Sleep taking him is like the seas closing over his head . . . panic and fear surge through his mind and body—and in that seam between waking and dreaming, the blankets feel like a giant hand closing around his entire body.

It feels completely real, though he *knows* it's not. He's being dragged down down *down* . . .

This isn't real! he thinks again. In crushing, suffocating confusion, Anton wriggles in the grasp of what his brain tells him are huge fingers, slime-covered and sticky: a zombie the size of a tyrannosaur, with teeth as big as tombstones—

This is the end. Anton is certain. But the next thing he knows, he comes awake in a knot of blankets, his heartbeat fast and hard . . .

Gradually the thumping slows.

The covers loosen.

The flood of fear gives way.

You're still alive, Anton thinks. Relief comes as sensation returns, courses through his numb arms and legs.

It lasts for as long as it takes Anton to remember what happened to Alek. And then the relief transforms . . .

A mixture of guilt and anger rises to the surface of his mind, like an oil spill that coats everything it touches.

He and Alek were *both* standing side by side when the zombie reached its hand out and ripped Alek's life away. There is no reason why Alek is gone and Anton isn't.

There's no sense to it.

In the darkness, Anton turns to the bedside table and opens the drawer, taking out the half deck of cards that he had in his pocket from that unfinished game of slap. Thirty-one cards, waterlogged and worn. Anton still carries them around, even though it's been three months since Alek died.

"Pick up your cards," Anton says as if his cousin were there, in the room.

This game will never end. He hears Alek's words rattle in his head, from that last day. Perhaps a memory—or perhaps a spirit that still lingers.

Anton isn't sure if he believes in that sort of thing.

He stands up and goes to the window. Pulling back the stuffy, light-blocking curtains, he peeks out—

Even though the clock reads three fifteen in the morning, he sees an incredible pink dawning sky. Such is the eerie glory of summer in the town of Munivit, Alaska: It's light out nearly twenty-four hours a day. Unlike the winter, when the sun barely drifts above the horizon.

And at the fringe of the night like this, Anton gets this tingling feeling—for a moment, sometimes he can sense Alek out there, somewhere.

But this is not one of those moments.

Today, Anton hears the very real sound of his front door opening and closing, followed by different voices: his brother Oz, his cousin Misha, and his father.

"So. What do you guys think?" says Oz, just a little too loud.

"What do we think of what?" says Anton's father. "And keep it down, Mom's asleep."

"What do you think we're *building*?" asks Oz.

"I think I'm too tired from *doing* the work to *think* about the work right now," says Misha. "Is it really still Monday?"

"Technically it's Tuesday morning," Anton's father says. "Also, we're not supposed to talk about what's going on inside the factory, Oz. Don't get us fired. The kind of money they're paying? This is the first good thing to happen to us in . . . It's possible this is the first good thing to *ever* happen to us. This time next year, the Zarkovskys will be back on the water where we belong, in a brand-new trawler."

"Not *all* of us," Anton mumbles to himself.

Dishes clatter in the kitchen for a while after that. A meal is being prepared. They're all just getting home from their new jobs, working second shift—late into the night—at a factory outside town.

"I think we're manufacturing rockets," Oz says. "Those rockets on the news. From California."

"You mean Cloudbusters?" says Misha.

"Those—yeah," Oz agrees. "The ones that can create a storm. Wipe out an entire zombie wave. Completely extinguished."

"That's a big leap, Ozzie," says Anton's father. "What makes you think—?"

"It makes sense, doesn't it?" Oz interrupts. "With all the hustle and secrecy up here?"

"He's got a point," says Misha. "Expanding the factory, all the people coming and going . . . Helicopters and planes and boats, all hours of the day and night?"

"And the new road they built for the big trucks?" adds Oz. "Plus, what better place to build them than up here, with the nice cool climate?"

Anton thinks about this for a moment, and he wants Oz to be right. He feels a surge of pride at the idea of his family, his community, being at the core of something so important.

Anton's so focused that he's caught by surprise by a sneeze.

He stifles it at the last second by thinking of a pineapple—which is the weirdest trick in the world, but it actually works . . . but Misha has ears like a bat and can tell Anton's there, listening at his bedroom door.

"Anton's up," says Misha.

"Anton?" his father calls. "Come on down if you're awake, be part of the family."

"Coming," says Anton, trudging to the kitchen.

"And by family I mean conspiracy," his father adds. "Please, Ozzie. Do me a favor and just focus on doing the work. Don't start rumors . . . even if they're totally right."

"So you believe it, Uncle Pete?" Misha asks. "We're making Cloudbusters. Right here in Munivit."

Anton's father doesn't answer.

"It makes a lot of sense to me," Anton says, coming into the kitchen. "And it's no fair you guys get to have all the fun without me."

Anton's father lowers his voice, serious. "We really shouldn't be talking about this stuff. The project leader is super paranoid about spies stealing his designs and copying the company's work."

"See? That's the problem," Oz says, brushing off his father's concern. "Sky Stone thinks the whole world's out to get him. If he's this big savior of humanity, why does he keep it all so private and exclusive all the time? Zombies are a problem for *everyone*, but *he's* more interested in protecting a profit."

"Do you really think Cloudbusters can get rid of zombies?" Anton asks quietly.

No one answers right away.

Misha looks at Anton and slowly puts together his thoughts. After a moment, he says, "It's complicated, I think."

"Eggs," Anton's father announces, putting a bowl on the kitchen counter, full of steaming hot, fluffy scrambled eggs. He's always been like this— taking care of everyone around him, no matter how tired he is. But ever since Alek's death, Anton's father has been even more dedicated. Anton never sees him rest anymore.

Anton is quietly determined to follow his father's lead. Never wasting a moment, not even a single breath. To live not only for himself but for his family . . . for Alek, most of all.

He can feel the emptiness every day. It's hard, living without all that thoughtfulness and care that Alek shared with Anton . . . the constant presence of adventure and joy that was always right there beside him. And Anton is determined to keep his cousin's spirit alive.

But as the family sits together and eats, there's a sound almost like an earthquake. An impact that rumbles the ground under the house, shaking the foundations.

They all look at one another, and quickly rise.

"Is it the glacier?" asks Misha.

"Get everybody up," says Anton's father. "Now!"

Misha and Oz exchange a look and then split up in opposite directions— Oz moving into the house, Misha out the front door.

"What about me?" says Anton.

"You're coming with me, buddy." Anton's father grabs him tight and pulls him toward the front door.

"What's happening?" says Anton.

Outside the house, Anton turns to look in the direction of the Munivit glacier, which has always loomed over the town like a low mountain.

But there's something very wrong about the wall of ice today. There's a giant crack in it. And from that crack emerges a zombie abomination. A giant, exactly like the one that haunts his nightmares. But this one is even bigger, and it's on land.

This is real, Anton thinks to himself with extreme dread.

7

DEADWOOD

Ruined buildings surround Chief Wachs's car as it rumbles onto the highway off-ramp for Redwood, which is marked with an orange sign reading EXIT CLOSED. It's followed by other signs: OFFICIAL VEHICLES ONLY . . . WELCOME TO DEADWOOD . . . Okay, that last one was clearly kids spray-painting over the old WELCOME TO REDWOOD sign so it reads "dead" instead of "red."

For Oliver, heading home to Redwood again is very weird and confusing. He thought it would be like fresh air in his lungs. Proof that life is going back to normal. But it's not. It's like falling asleep for a nap and waking up to discover a hundred years have passed.

The closer he gets to Redwood, the farther away home seems.

"Someone's gonna fix the sign, right, Aunt C?" Oliver asks his aunt.

Chief Wachs glances at the rearview mirror, looking back at Oliver.

"Eyes on your own work, Ollie," she says. "This isn't a game. This isn't fun. This is community service you and your friends volunteered for. Let's not forget that being here is a privilege. No shenanigans."

"Yes, Chief," says Del in the front seat. He has been sitting so quietly that

Oliver keeps forgetting his best friend has been there this whole time. He's trying to convince Chief Wachs he's ready for duty.

"Good to be back, right, Del?" says Kirby brightly.

Del shrugs. "Home sweet home . . ."

Kirby looks like she wants to say something else, but she stops herself. She makes a sour face as she glances at Oliver.

Oliver and Kirby have grown more and more worried about how the soft-spoken, bighearted Del has suddenly dedicated himself to becoming a zombiefighter. And the way that he's trying to impress Chief Wachs with how devoted he is isn't helping. He's rigid in his seat, like a soldier. Like a machine.

Oliver vividly remembers the last time he and Del were in Redwood: in the Wachs family minivan, fists of zombies pummeling them on all sides . . . lost in panic amidst all that chaos and fear . . .

But now things are different. For Del, and for Redwood.

As more and more of the city drifts past the window, Oliver starts to feel a little panicked, too. The wrecked areas are worse than ever, overtaken by coyotes and vultures. But even the new construction is upsetting to Oliver. His gaze lingers on a half-built, hulking block of town houses, with a wall around it, and a channel for a moat beyond that. It looks more like a castle than a community.

A completely different place than the Redwood he loves, that's for sure.

In the entire valley, pretty much the only things that *haven't* changed at all are the enormous coastal sequoias. The redwood trees that have been here for hundreds and hundreds of years—the fury of the zombie horde left scars on the bark, but damaged little else.

Downtown remains more familiar to Oliver, thanks to the zombie brigade's hard-won battle at the bridge. But the resulting damage to the area is shocking to see:

Giant machines are tearing down the remains of the collapsed bridge, and others are sucking everything out of the riverbed. They're trying to sift out all the zombie bodies that fell in, Chief Wachs explains, to guard against the possibility that one might reemerge. But the cost of this safety is clear to Oliver. Nothing undead will lurk in the river . . . but nothing alive will remain, either.

What if Del's actually right? Oliver starts to wonder. Even if Redwood is rebuilt, what if their home *is* gone forever?

Oliver pushes this thought away and tries very hard to forget it.

He has a job to do. Regina already sent him her location and expects him to sneak away and find her, but he's not sure how *that's* going to happen quite yet. He just keeps focused, eyes and ears open. Regina's counting on him to secretly map the zombie tunnels she'll need, to fight back against the company that's *really* the enemy right now. Or so she insists.

You're ready for the mission, he tries to convince himself as Chief Wachs pulls the car into a parking lot that's full of official vehicles and construction equipment. The other ZDP kids Del got to come are in a second car that pulls up a moment later. Milo's dad is driving, with Milo in the passenger seat and four other kids in the back, including Chanda and Darlene. Not Conrad, though.

Chief Wachs turns off the engine and calls out, "Okay, kids! You ready?"

"Let's take out the trash, Chief," says Del, hopping out of the car. Carrying himself like a loyal brigadier, he eagerly follows Chief Wachs. She takes a giant roll of black trash bags from the trunk and hands them out.

"More like bring *in* the trash," says Kirby, brandishing a long pole with a two-prong grabber on the end.

"Let's clean this place up so we can get back to normal life," says Oliver, accepting a trash bag, too.

"Or at least we'll end up with some really good zombie counter-measures," says Del.

"Zombie countermeasures?" says Kirby.

"Decoys," Milo explains to Kirby. "When you're on the run from a zombie, a bag of trash can work as a decoy to distract them long enough for you to make an escape."

"It can also be used for bait," Del adds. "Pile up a lot of trash, and use it to lure an entire horde into a trap, where you soak 'em with superchillers!"

"Okay, listen up," says Chief Wachs. "Here are the conditions of your visit to the Redwood disaster recovery zone: While we're here, you don't argue with me, even a little, understand? And if I say to do something, you *do it* right away, and we can discuss *why* later. Capisce?"

"Yes, ma'am!" Del answers, like a soldier. "Let's do the job and get back home!"

Chief Wachs looks at the others expectantly. "Capisce, Oliver?"

"Capisce."

"Capisce, Kirby?"

"Aye aye, Aunt C."

"Milo?"

"What's 'ka-peesh' mean?" Milo asks, sounding out the unfamiliar word.

Chief Wachs stares at Milo. "I see you're gonna be the troublemaker today."

"Just say capisce," Oliver whispers.

"I just asked what it *means*," Milo counters. "You shouldn't agree to things you don't fully understand, Ollie."

"This way, everyone!" Chief Wachs and Milo's father lead Oliver, Kirby, Del, and the others along a series of eerily empty streets—areas deemed clear of zombies and safe to use, but with all other rubble and wreckage untouched.

As the others talk, Oliver opens the Mapmaker Alpha app on his phone and secretly begins his real task, mapping the strangely unfamiliar features of his hometown. Seeking pathways not shown on regular maps. So Regina will be able to escape the spying eyes of HumaniTeam as she looks for proof that they're not the heroes everyone thinks they are.

Consulting his phone, Oliver moves in Regina's direction, eyes scanning everywhere.

As he glances around, he has to settle his breath. There it is. A ragged-looking opening in the ground, covered with a piece of wreckage that looks like it was once the roof of someone's shed.

It's one of the tunnels the zombies left behind, Oliver knows. An opening to what Regina says is their network of caves.

But as he slips away from the others and moves a little closer, Oliver freezes—caught completely unprepared by the sight of two pinpricks of orange staring back at him.

Eyes.

A zombie.

And Oliver can sense that he's already been seen.

NIX

The boy is delivering himself right into Nix's grasp.

The superheated blood in his inhuman veins urges him forward with the hunger of a starving animal.

Free of his captivity in the basement, there's nothing stopping him from feeding now. He could attack and take the living completely by surprise. In a moment he would be strong and powerful once more. And his zombie body trembles with its eagerness to hunt. To greedily consume.

"Stay calm, Nix," says Regina Herrera, almost silently. Her hand is on a banged-up emergency extinguisher she pilfered from the HumaniTeam office.

He battles the urges inside himself, because Nix isn't exactly like the others of his kind. Despite his zombie appearance, part of his mind is awake again. All that time in HumaniTeam's lab, when his mind was trained. Ruthlessly trained to strategize and plan—

For Nix, it's easy to see the future that would lie ahead if he fed as all zombies instinctively do. Regina would be forced to try and extinguish him, of course.

But even more than that . . . he'd be alone again. Alone, forever.

That, more than anything, Nix could not bear.

So from inside the cave, the half human, half zombie just watches Oliver.

Unblinking. Completely focused.

"We're going to help you, Nix," Regina continues. "Oliver, too. Even if he doesn't know that quite yet."

". . . Plan?" says Nix, his voice a barely audible croak.

Regina nods, understanding. "Plan. Right. First? We're going to get you somewhere safe. Away from the clutches of HumaniTeam. But we *can't* be seen. Bad things will happen to you if they catch us. And you can be sure they're watching somehow. You'll end up right back in some secret lab, probably. If you're not extinguished right away, that is. So you need to trust us, okay? Me *and* Oliver. You're going to go with him to safety. And I'll join you as soon as I can. And then I'll tell you what you're going to do for me in return."

Nix watches her as she watches him so fiercely.

He wonders what Regina's really up to. Why is she helping him? What does she want from Nix?

But before he can summon the right words to ask, she stands and heads off toward Oliver.

To Nix's surprise, he's curious.

It's a feeling that he hasn't had for a very, very long time.

9

ABOMINATION

As Anton and his father clamber into a rusty, ancient pickup truck, Misha sprints down the street to the house where the rest of the Zarkovsky clan lives. Aunt Beth and Uncle K. All of Anton's cousins and his grandmother. Meanwhile, Oz and Anton's other brothers rush outside, scrambling to get into their father's truck. Squeezing into the cab, climbing into the bed.

Anton's mother pauses on the porch, looking out, counting heads. She looks relieved until she turns in the direction of the cousins' house.

Anton follows her gaze. Something's wrong.

There's no one outside yet.

"Dad?" says Anton, pointing to the other house.

Just at that moment, Misha comes back outside—alone.

"Uncle Pete!" calls Misha.

"What's wrong?" Anton's mother calls to Misha.

"She's refusing to come, she thinks—she thinks . . ."

Anton hears his grandmother's voice emerge from the open front door. "Alek! Alek?" she shouts.

"Grandma, we have to go," Misha pleads.

"We're not leaving without Alek," Anton's grandmother insists.

She doesn't remember Alek's gone, Anton realizes.

"How *could* you, Peter?" his grandma demands, stepping outside, looking right at Misha. His grandmother's memory has been getting worse amidst all her grief over Alek's death. She's mixing up the names of her family, too, thinking Misha is her son, not her grandson. It's hard for Anton to watch.

And in the pickup truck, watching is all Anton can do. Anton looks to his father, and he sees how much this hurts him, too. Her raw emotion reopens a wound that can't fully heal. *We lost Alek. We didn't react quick enough, smart enough. And then it was too late to do anything. And now . . . Alek's gone.*

Meanwhile, the earth under them rumbles and Anton's head swivels.

His eyes trace the seaside bluffs that jut up from the ocean like strong shoulders, prickling with pine trees. And down the long, winding street he lives on, cradled in the valley between those bluffs, everyone else is just as confused as Anton, it seems. Every household is in various states of shock and reaction.

Then Anton's eyes move finally to the mountain-like wall of rocky ice that's loomed over the town for his entire life—the Munivit glacier, for which the town is named.

Today, the wall of ice has a giant crack in it. Like a jail cell broken open . . .

But the zombie that emerged is nowhere in sight. And it's actually more nerve-wracking that way—not knowing where it is . . .

As Anton looks around, wild-eyed, he notices his father locking eyes with his mother. She nods in response and streaks toward Uncle K and Aunt Beth's house. Meanwhile, Anton's father throws the car into gear.

Despite the jerky motion, Anton pulls out his phone and aims the camera, zooming in to see more detail than he can with his unassisted eye.

Giant footprints, each of them as large as the pickup truck in which Anton sits, trace a path out of the cavelike darkness of the glacier's interior. Crushing rock and ice as easily as bare feet in the sandy beach.

As Anton's father reverses down the driveway too fast for comfort, the pickup truck groans in protest of all the weight of Oz, Anton, and their brothers.

Anton steadies the camera as much as he can as they head down the driveway, and peers at what they're running from. A trail of destruction becomes clear as Anton tracks the giant footprints: Tree trunks ripped from stumps and devoured. Cabins along the peaceful banks of the water pulled down, cracked open like eggs plucked from a carton. A bed afloat in the water, buffeted between the white water and the constant tide . . .

Anton wonders whether there was a person peacefully sleeping in there only moments ago . . . at least he does for a fleeting moment, until the cause of all the destruction comes into view.

The zombie abomination, flesh swollen, as wide as it is tall. Round as the ever-spinning Earth, but with only a bottomless hunger at its core.

They've come face-to-face with such a nightmare once before, in the middle of the ocean. That one was algae-covered, gently glowing with green-yellow bioluminescence, and somehow slimy and sticky at the same time. Oddly, this one seems both older and newly awakened.

Its hunger seems sharper, too.

"Dad?" says Anton. He taps his father on the shoulder and points.

"I see it," Anton's father says with no emotion in his voice at all.

How was this ever a human being? Anton wonders in horror and disbelief.

It shouldn't be possible. Anton cannot imagine the forces that turn people into zombies and zombies into . . . this. A monster that towers above the trees. Anton feels a rush of fear as it charges right at his zoomed-in camera lens.

But then he looks at it without the camera, and it's far in the distance.

Keep calm, take precautions, stay safe. Anton remembers what he's been taught. He wonders if it'll make a difference.

At the bottom of the driveway, Anton's father crosses paths with the neighbors, Emi and Clea. Anton's father asks if they need help and they ask him the same in their turn, looking down the street to the chaos at Aunt Beth and Uncle K's.

"We should all stick together, I think," says Anton, even though no one was asking for his input.

Anton and his father look at each other, an unspoken pain in the air.

"No one gets left behind this time," Anton's father agrees. He suggests to Emi and Clea that they all should drive in a caravan, protecting each other. As Emi nods, grateful for this, Anton's father grasps the gearshift and works the clutch and the gas—

Anton can almost feel the spirit of Alek in the car with them. A fresh hope, a ray of sun.

Alek would be proud of Anton's choice just then, he believes.

He knows it, and it makes him feel like he hasn't *completely* lost his cousin and best friend. Every choice Anton makes now is a chance for Alek to live on a little longer. Every brave or thoughtful thing Anton does makes Alek more a part of the world.

As the pickup truck races down the uneven road, Anton feels cold and numb. He feels adrift in all the chaos. Like in his nightmare, bobbing in the sea. He clutches the deck of cards in his pocket, settling himself. *Focus on what's happening right now, Anton*, he tells himself. *Do something to help.*

Unlike in California and other areas closer to civilization, there are no evacuation routes or permanent sirens here to warn of zombie danger. There's only one road, after all. And people are too far apart for sirens to be effective.

Zombies have always been a welter of orange eyes and suffocating heat, leaving a trail of destroyed forests and towns. What does it mean that there are now giants emerging from *icy glaciers*? It's too much to make sense of.

The world is breaking.

Despite Anton's fear, he borrows Alek's courage, and makes a choice to keep watch as keenly as any lookout.

And it makes all the difference, because Anton notices something about the way the zombie is moving that's unexpected and revealing:

The zombie is pretty closely following the flow of the water from the glacier to the sea.

And every time it strays, racing up the banks to uproot a tree or split open a cabin, it starts to lose strength fast. To deflate and dwindle in size.

"It has to stay near the water," he says out loud.

"What's that?" Anton's father asks.

"Dad, I think it has to stay near the water. I don't think it can come onto dry land."

"You *think*?" He looks at Anton, clearly not wanting to grapple with any new surprises.

"Dad! What do you want from me?"

Anton's father swallows his frustration and claps his hand onto Anton's shoulder. "Thanks, Anton."

Anton's father glances in the rearview mirror quickly, seeing the long line of other vehicles trailing behind.

With a sudden exhale, Anton's father presses the brakes, bringing the car to a stop in the middle of the road.

Behind him, the other families brake, too.

Clea and Emi poke their heads out of their open windows.

"What happened?" they ask.

"Back it up, folks!" Anton's father calls to them. "That thing can't come onto dry land, we think, which means we need to turn this thing around and head up-country!"

"You *think*?" says Clea.

But Clea and Emi look back at the zombie and their expressions change. They shout to the car behind them—or ahead of them, as things now stand—

"You *THINK*?" yells another driver, farther up the road.

As the cars turn around, Anton sits as still as a statue in his seat.

"What if this doesn't work?" Anton asks his father.

"You live and you learn," his father tells him with a shrug. "No shortcut around it."

"Emphasis on *live*," says Anton nervously.

10

DEADWOOD, PART 2

As Regina moves silently toward Oliver, she sees his eyes are wide open, trained on the darkness of the tunnel where Nix is waiting. She sneaks up and whispers beside his ear, "Oliver Wachs!"

"Regina?!" he says, jumping in shock. His reaction goes from furious to relieved and back again.

"Surprise surprise," says Regina, dryly.

"Don't do that. I thought you were a zombie."

"Why would you think that?" she says, keenly aware of the others nearby. "No zombies here."

"Look, in the tunnel," he whispers. "There's a z—"

Regina gives Oliver a warning look. "There's nothing dangerous in the tunnels, Ollie," she says, shushing him with a finger to her lips. She eyes the other kids, who are taking notice nearby. "Not that a kid like me would know anything about any secret zombie-made subway system under Redwood."

"If you say so," says Oliver. "I'm working on a map right now, like you asked."

"That's good to hear," says Regina. "But . . . we have a change of plans, actually."

"Change of plans?" Oliver asks. "You don't need a map of the tunnels anymore?"

"I needed that a week ago," says Regina. "What I need now is a little bigger."

Oliver lowers his eyes, like he's embarrassed. But Regina didn't mean for him to feel bad. She's just focused on the job. Getting Nix away from here.

"I found it, Oliver," she says, brimming with excitement. "I've got proof. Walking, talking proof that HumaniTeam aren't the big heroes they pretend to be. I can expose them, and stop the Cloudbuster launches. But I need your help to sneak him out of Redwood undetected."

"Okay, back up," says Oliver. "You need to start again. Way back. The whole HumaniTeam equals bad thing—you actually found proof that Cloudbusters are creating the zombies?"

"Making them immune to water, to be precise."

"And you're sure they *know* it's happening?" he asks.

Regina nods. "They're lying to everyone to protect themselves. Their profit."

Oliver frowns, still unhappy. "Okay, well . . . people need to see your proof, I guess," he says. "But what exactly does 'sneak *him* out of Redwood' mean?"

"One thing at a time," says Regina, eyes scanning the area, seeing two other kids approaching—a girl and a boy. Unhappily, she asks, "What's the deal with all your friends?"

"Oh, uh," Oliver stumbles. "Regina, this is Del Shorter. Del, this is Regina Herrera—"

"You're Regina?" the girl interrupts. "Hey! I'm Ollie's sister, Kirby Wachs. I've heard so much about you . . ."

"Hi." Regina brushes Kirby aside. "Ollie. Why did you bring all these people?"

"Gimme a break, Regina, it wasn't exactly easy to convince my aunt to bring me," Oliver complains.

"Okay, okay, whatever. I need to talk to you."

"So *talk.*"

"Alone, Oliver." Regina frowns. "I trust *you.* But all these other people . . . ?"

But before she can go on, an adult voice interrupts. "I didn't know you were joining us today, Regina."

Frustrated, Regina turns.

"Chief Wachs," says Regina with a plastered-on smile. She wracks her brain for an excuse to get out of the cleanup detail, but fails to come up with anything.

"You know me, Chief," Regina says. "Always happy to help."

"Well, then. Welcome to the cleanup crew." She hands Regina a spare trash bag.

"Thanks, Chief," says Regina, resigned.

From the mouth of the cave, she meets Nix's gaze, and urges him to stay and wait as Kirby, Del, Milo, and the others all continue to fill bag after bag of trash and deposit them in their wake at the curb. It barely makes a dent in all the chaos surrounding them.

"Stay close, everyone!" calls out Chief Wachs.

But the first chance Regina gets, she pulls Oliver away from the others. "Ollie! This way."

As she leads him back toward the tunnel where she left Nix, Oliver starts pestering her for answers. "What's going *on*, Regina?" Oliver demands. "I definitely saw a zombie in here before."

"I know, Ollie," says Regina. "He's with me."

"He's with you?" Oliver repeats. "Hold on. *Hold on.*"

"Oliver . . ."

"Walking proof . . ." Oliver says. "Oh no. Is *he* your proof HumaniTeam is bad?"

Regina sighs. "Yes."

"Regina!"

"He's not what you think!" Regina tells him.

"What is he, then?" Oliver asks, frowning.

"Okay, he is what you think," Regina admits.

"Talk, Regina. You want me to team up with a *zombie* . . . over the people who *save the world* from zombies?"

"I told you: They aren't *saving* the world," says Regina. "HumaniTeam has gone to extraordinary lengths to hide the truth that superchillers are actually making the zombies *much* worse. They're totally focused on their big dreams, and they hide their failures so nobody ever blames them."

She closes her eyes to clear her head. As she does, she sees a flash of a mine shaft full of zombies. Project Coloma. The generator that her parents built—that Regina had the idea for. A disaster happened . . . and then the company tried to hide the disaster, but the zombies all got out and caused the Rogue Wave.

And then Kai rebuilt a mini-NRG to help her get access to HumaniTeam's computers . . . but Regina wasn't about to make a disastrous mistake twice. She went back, determined to shut it down. To disassemble the mini-NRG and sacrifice her own dreams of finding proof of Project Phoenix. But to her total surprise, going back to confront the problem actually led her *right* to the solution she'd been searching for high and low:

There, among the cage full of zombies—their nightmare, snake-jawed smiles; the hollow orange eyes—she found a familiar face. An individual caught in the gray area between the worlds of zombiehood and humanity. Nix.

She opens her eyes and considers Oliver nervously. Can she truly trust him?

"You have to promise to keep what I'm telling you secret, Oliver," Regina demands. "Between us. Nobody else."

"Fine," says Oliver. "You saved my life, I can keep a secret for you."

"Good. But I'm actually asking you for a little more than that," Regina presses.

"Regina, what is going on?" Oliver says, worried.

"Ollie, I'd like to introduce you to someone," says Regina. "His name is Nix."

At Regina's gesture, Nix himself steps out of a hiding place near the mouth of the tunnel.

Oliver gasps, tense. He immediately shifts to zombie-defense mode—

"Don't panic, Oliver," says Regina. But in her chest, she feels a pulse of adrenaline, too.

She isn't comfortable around Nix, despite how important he is to her plans. This is, after all, the zombie who wanted her to join his horde not very long ago. To be a greedy, soulless monster and stay with him, leading the zombie horde as a general leads an army.

But what Nix didn't understand is something every human being does: that friendship requires trust. It can't be taken, only given. And though she will not forgive him for his actions, to her surprise, she *is* glad he's not extinguished.

"Look, Ollie," says Regina. "We don't have much time, but I want you to know: I know I should've trusted you from the start. I'm sorry."

He looks distracted, fixated on Nix. "Trusted me with what?"

"Remember the first thing you ever said to me? The first conversation we ever had . . ."

"I remember being stuck up a tree," Oliver replies.

Regina nods. "And then you and I talked on the phone . . . and you asked me if I noticed that the zombies in Redwood were acting strangely? If I'd noticed them working together as a team? Acting smart?"

Oliver's expression changes. He remembers. "You *did* see it. Why did you pretend you didn't?"

"Because the truth is way worse than you think it is. The truth is that HumaniTeam experimented on zombies to see if they could *make* them smarter, Oliver. They actually succeeded."

Oliver gets very quiet. "Did you just say smart—*smart* zombies?"

Regina nods. "Nix was one of the experimental subjects. The name Nix is short for Phoenix, actually. And Project Phoenix is the code name for HumaniTeam's experiment to try and turn zombies into productive members of society. It didn't work out."

"Regina, that's . . . that's . . ."

Oliver is speechless.

"It's awful," Regina agrees. "HumaniTeam is really good at covering their tracks, but they didn't count on me and the Junior Zombie Brigade. We risked our lives to uncover what was really happening with Project Phoenix. How they wanted to create more zombies like Nix, make them into a workforce. The world needs to know. And that's what I need your help with. You need to hide him for me."

Oliver laughs. "Sorry, what?"

"HumaniTeam is watching me. I can't get him out of Redwood undetected. But you? You're here with the head of the zombie brigade," says Regina. "They won't suspect you."

"You want me to sneak a zombie out of Redwood how?"

"In the trunk of your aunt's car."

"Seriously? And then what?"

"And then take him back to Stuxville, and hide him until I can pick him up."

Oliver looks shocked. "How long?"

"A day, maybe two."

"No way."

"You *can* say no, Ollie," Regina tells him. "This isn't a small thing to ask."

"What happens if I say no?"

"Then the world goes on using Cloudbusters and the zombies keep getting stronger until it's too late to stop them. By the end of the summer, they could be totally invincible. Immune to superchillers. Supercharged, in fact."

"You're asking me to risk my family getting hurt, to protect a monster?"

"Nix won't hurt you," says Regina. "If you're not going to do it, tell me now."

Regina is surprised to discover that she almost *hopes* he says no. This whole half-baked plan of hers could spell disaster in so many ways . . . The idea of helping this half monster, half human regain his strength? Getting him on her side?

"You really believe we can do it, Regina?" Oliver asks. "Use this zombie to expose what HumaniTeam is doing?"

"We have to. And Nix could be an ally like we've never had before—and we'll never get this chance again," says Regina, even as she waffles and debates calling the whole thing off.

Oliver pulls himself up as tall as he can. "Okay," he says. "I'll help."

Regina feels a huge weight lift as Oliver agrees.

"You sure, Ollie?" she asks.

He nods. "It worked out okay last time, didn't it? I trust you."

Regina feels better right away, now that she has Oliver to count on.

"Okay, Ollie. Right now what we need is to come up with a way to distract the adults and get him into the trunk of your aunt's car."

A familiar feeling courses through her. It's a flowing confidence—an itchy instinct to take risks and keep pushing forward, at all costs. Further, faster, bigger. It's a feeling that, in the past, she hasn't had any ability to resist. Like a mosquito bite that seems to get harder and harder to ignore the more you scratch—

Down the back of her neck, she feels a tingle of warning. She remembers how Nix tried to get her to join him, back in Redwood. She has to be careful around him, she knows. She could lose more than her life.

But she takes a moment just to appreciate that thrill of widening possibility, through the buzz of exhaustion. It reminds her of being on that hilltop with Oliver, after surviving the Rogue Wave.

To her surprise, as she looks around, she realizes they're actually very close to where she and Oliver outraced death.

"Hey, come over here," says Regina.

She leads Oliver over a hill, to where the rubble that remains of the Redwood Zombie Brigade Headquarters can be seen. She points it out to Oliver. "We already saved Redwood once, remember? Right on this spot. We got the message out. We're alive. We just have to stick together."

Oliver takes a deep breath. "You're right. Thank you, Regina."

As his tension bleeds away, he spins around in a circle. Scanning the old trees, the ruined buildings, the transformed river—

An unexpected laugh bursts out of him.

"What's so funny, Ollie?"

"Everything! Smart zombies? This bizarre version of Redwood? When I got up this morning, I was nervous about messing up a map . . . but now here we are, and I have to hide a zombie from the company that's hunting him, or the world will surely be doomed. It's a little funny."

"A little, maybe," says Regina, feeling a laugh build inside her, too.

Luckily, they've stopped talking in the nick of time, because in the silence, Regina hears Chief Wachs's voice:

"There you are!" says Chief Wachs, marching up to them with a hand on her superchiller. "What did I tell you about staying close?!"

Oliver and Regina look at her wordlessly.

"This field trip is over," Chief Wachs barks. "Back to the car. Now."

As they head back, Oliver asks Regina, "Showtime?"

Regina watches Nix keep pace with them in the shadows.

She nods. "Showtime."

11

ABOMINATION, PART 2

Anton remains statue-still in the passenger seat of his father's truck as the enormous zombie thunders across the landscape. Meanwhile, the cars that were following the Zarkovskys' truck in a long line struggle to make U-turns and head back the way they came.

That means the Zarkovskys are at the *end* of the caravan of cars now, not in the lead. All they can do is sit and wait.

Anton's muscles are rigid . . . He's even holding his breath. All his attention is focused on willing the zombie not to notice them. To stay near the frothy white water released by the glacier, which it seems to require to stay strong. So Anton *believes*, anyway.

From a long way up the line of cars, Anton hears another distant voice call out, "What do you mean *'you think'* it can't come on dry land?"

Anton swallows hard.

From the driver's seat, Anton's father reaches out to grasp Anton's shoulder.

"There's no one around who knows any more than *you*, Anton. You figured something out, and told someone who could help. That's a good day's work. If we're wrong? We'll be wrong together. We'll deal with it."

The other vehicles in the caravan all continue slowly turning around and heading back uphill the way they came, without the zombie giving chase. But even though it's the Zarkovskys' turn, Anton's dad doesn't move.

He watches the behemoth in the gushing white water.

Thinking.

"Dad?" says Anton.

Anton follows his father's gaze a little farther and realizes that he's not watching where the zombie *is*—he's watching where it's *going*.

Anton sees the engorged river tumble over the bluffs to the harbor below.

The harbor that's been packed full of supply ships ever since work at the factory went into overdrive.

"The supply ships . . ." says Anton. "The crews are all down there."

"I know, Anton." His father has his phone to his ear and it's ringing.

"Are you calling the harbormaster?"

"Trying," says Anton's father.

As it rings and rings, his father gets exasperated. He hangs up and makes a second call. "Pick up, guys."

The second call rings and rings, too.

"We're not leaving them behind. Right, Dad?" asks Anton.

"I'm working on it, buddy."

He calls a third number.

Anton's heart is in his throat. What will they do if no one down there answers their phone?

As if Anton's question resonates in the air, Anton's father revs the engine, getting ready to race down to the seaport, even though it means putting themselves closer to the zombie kaiju.

Anton takes out his phone and zooms in to see the enormous abominable no-man moving faster now than before.

The zombie is almost racing toward the ocean.

Ignoring everything in its path—there's something that's got its total focus. Something drawing it *away* from the seaport.

A vehicle that Anton can't quite make out. A blur of speed. He starts recording video of what he's watching.

It's an ATV of some kind, he thinks. With two people in it, though he can't really make out much of who they are. He gets out of the car, where the windshield isn't in the way. He expertly adjusts the controls of the camera to get a little better result—

There's a woman driving, it looks like. A man with a short white beard is in the other seat. And . . . and . . . for some reason there's a *giant rocket* strapped to the top. A rocket that's leaking white gas that blows backward in the turbulence behind it.

As Anton focuses on these details, the zombie catches its prey, and Anton gasps. It rips the rocket clean off the ATV.

"Look, Dad!" Anton says, pointing.

"I don't know what you're showing me, Anton," Anton's father says. He's finally reached someone at the seaport and is talking serious and fast.

Anton continues to record the encounter.

The zombie breaks the rocket open.

Ice crystals grow on the zombie and everything the gas touches.

A Cloudbuster rocket, it must be.

His brother Oz was right: The factory his family is working at is manufacturing *Cloudbusters!*

"You need to tell them *not* to sail," says Anton's father. "Tell them the thing can't come on dry land, tell them to get *off* the boats—"

Anton just watches the zombie devour the rocket. It makes all the veins in the zombie's body pulse and turn icy blue. And as it does, the woman driving the ATV stands up, holding something that looks like a grappling hook attached to a cable.

She flings it at the zombie, and it flies far over the target, but then she *pulls* and the hook sets in the zombie's shoulder, like a fishhook.

As the woman reaches for something in the ATV, the zombie suddenly flinches in irritation.

It tries to reach for the cable tethered to the hook in its shoulder, but then a second flinch turns into a spasm—

A *shock*. An electric shock, Anton realizes.

Impossibly, Anton thinks they're trying to fight the zombie.

But the zombie rages and charges toward the bluffs along the water. The ATV, still tethered to it with the hook, accelerates to give chase.

Right at the bluff.

"No no no—" Anton says.

"That's Vic," says Anton's father, now watching Anton's phone screen, too. Transfixed. "That's Vic Pinkerton. And—"

His father falters and gasps as the raging zombie charges at the bluffs and leaps off, plummeting into the ocean. Attached to the zombie by that cable, the ATV is pulled off the cliff, too.

Out of sight.

Anton instantly shuts off the camera, realizing what he just witnessed.

His heart thumps like he's running at top speed. His father's gone quiet and pale.

Moment after moment passes.

Anton can't move. His limbs feel too heavy.

And then the zombie reappears at the seaport below.

"Come away, Anton," his father says.

They both know what comes next now, as the zombie focuses its attention on a large supply ship. Tearing, punching, clawing—making a hole in the boat so it can get inside.

On the opposite side of the vessel, people leap off the boat, into the water.

Anton remembers exactly what that was like. He feels it every night when he's falling asleep.

He can't move at all.

"Anton."

He can't look away.

". . . Anton, let's go."

Anton feels his father attempting to get his attention, but ignores it. He lifts the phone again, zooming in to see—to see something he doesn't believe.

And yet? There it is.

"Dad," he croaks. "Look."

Anton makes sure he's recording again: On the phone screen, zoomed the whole way in, Anton can make out a speeding thing whipping around the zombie. And he can *just* make out two people in it—

"It's them!" says Anton. On the screen of Anton's phone, the little ATV zips on the surface of the water like a Jet Ski.

It really is an *all-terrain* vehicle.

The zombie ignores this entirely, intensely focused on what it's doing. On prying open the cargo hold of the ship. It's blind to everything else— animal, plant, or human—in its path.

"Dad, who is that? You *know* them?"

The cable towed by the ATV winds around the zombie again and again, tightening. Pinning the zombie's arms to its sides as it devours what looks like another rocket.

Ice crystals grow on the rocket's shell and the zombie's skin as the zombie swallows it greedily. White gas leaks out of its open jaws . . .

In the zombie's belly, a chemical reaction is happening. First, the belly distends, like a snake that's just fed, swallowing its prey whole.

Then the awful, sludge-filled veins harden all along the zombie's skin—turning sapphire blue and standing out against the raw, angry flesh.

With incredible fury, the zombie flexes its strength to break free of the taut cord, but there's a sudden blinding white light, and Anton flinches away.

Anton watches the rest without the help of the phone's magnification.

The zombie goes rigid. The powerful jaw muscles clench so hard that teeth would break if the thing were still human.

For a second time, the world blazes white. And this time, Anton recognizes it for what it is: an electric shock—something like lightning is running through the giant zombie, conducted by the cable, like a Taser.

Unable to control its body, it starts to topple.

The body of the monster has already been shackled using the strongest cables available when Anton and his father arrive at the seaport.

"You did it!" Anton calls out. "You saved Munivit!"

Vic Pinkerton, the woman, who is dressed like a superhero in a thick, tightly fitting rubber garment, nods for a security person to come over. But before that happens, Anton crows, "And *I* got it *all!*" and the man with the shock of windswept white hair and beard, Sky Stone, cocks his head a little.

Turning to Anton, he asks, "What's that?"

Anton's smile only grows wider. "All the action, the whole thing . . . I got it on video! Everyone's gonna know what you did. That you're heroes."

Sky Stone smiles at Anton, but there's no warmth behind it. Just steel strength. Anton's never met someone like this before.

Anton feels his father's arm on his shoulder. "Anton! There you are. You *cannot* run away like that. I need to get to work, and so do they. Get back in the truck and wait for me. Sorry, Mr. Stone."

Anton is pulled away.

Back in the truck, he watches as a helicopter rushes to hover over one of the piers nearby. Below it, Anton's father is part of the team helping to evacuate a group of injured people. People who got pulled from the water. Half drowned and half electrocuted.

Anton swallows his excitement about the day's heroic events: It's not that simple, he can see.

That's when he hears his name. "Zarkovsky."

He turns, and sees Vic Pinkerton walking up to the truck Anton's sitting inside.

"Yes, ma'am? Can I help you?"

"*Can* you help me? Let's find out."

And then, as Pinkerton goes on talking, Anton kind of short-circuits from excitement.

But at the end of the conversation, he's given the woman all the videos he took, and erased them from his phone. Vic Pinkerton tells Anton that Sky Stone thinks there's a future for him with the company one day. And that, if Anton wants, Sky has an idea for a good place to start.

12

DEADWOOD, PART 3

On the drive back to Stuxville, Oliver tenses as they go over every pothole and around every turn.

There's a zombie in the trunk, after all.

Oliver didn't get a clear look at Nix when Regina was sneaking him through the tunnels and smuggling him into the car. He was much too busy using all the resources at his disposal to pull off this truly unthinkable feat. If it weren't for Regina's fierce support, he would've admitted he was in over his head. But he could tell that this wasn't something to mess around with. He wants the thing out of the trunk and locked up tight until Regina can come to collect him.

It will take several days for her to sort that out, apparently.

"Where am I going to hide a zombie for *several days*, Regina?" he asked her.

"Figure it out" was all she said.

He had no choice. Not anymore. That moment had passed.

"I can't do this alone," Oliver quickly realized.

"Tell whoever you trust," Regina said, surprising Oliver.

"Really?"

"We're gonna need all the friends we can get if we're going to stand up to HumaniTeam," Regina explained. "But if our secret gets out, I'll know it's *your* fault."

Right away, Oliver went to talk to Del. But as he thought about it more, he hesitated.

Across the back seat of the car, he looks at Kirby and gets her attention. He slips her his notebook, in which he's written a message for her.

As she reads it, she looks at her brother in confusion.

He gestures for her to keep reading.

She turns the page and her eyes widen. She doesn't look up at him right away. She just . . . reads.

And then she looks up at Oliver and gives a tiny nod.

Oliver hates that he's getting her involved in this. It's his job as the older sibling to protect her, after all. But when he looks at Del in the front passenger seat, he can't help but feel that anything he tells Del, he's also telling the whole group of ZDP kids.

Kirby closes the notebook and hands it back to Oliver.

She gestures for him to open it. He does, and sees she's added a note for Oliver.

It just says, *Library. Room B4.*

Oliver raises an eyebrow. *Not really sure if that's a good idea.*

She stares back. *You got a better one?*

They ride in tense silence the rest of the journey back to Stuxville. As the car approaches the campus, Oliver can feel his heart start to race.

No time to turn back now.

"Aunt Carrie?" asks Kirby. "Can you come in for dinner, maybe?"

"Sadly, I have a lot more work to do still today," says Chief Wachs.

"Oh," says Kirby. "Okay. Sorry."

Oliver feels his heart race faster. Is that it? *What are you doing, Kirby?*

Kirby ignores Oliver, staring out the window blankly.

Oliver is starting to freak out—they *need* Aunt Carrie to leave the car long enough so he can quietly move the zombie in the trunk! But just as he's about to interrupt, he catches his aunt watching Kirby in the rearview mirror.

"Oh, all right," says Chief Wachs. "Don't be so *dramatic.*"

Kirby looks from her aunt to her brother, wearing a smile equal parts mischief and sweetness the whole time. *Watch and learn, big brother.*

As Chief Wachs parks the car and everyone gets out, she pulls Oliver aside.

"Hey, Ollie," she says. "Sorry for cutting the day short. You had a good one today, kid. It takes a lot of work to start rebuilding something. Laying that foundation is an extraordinarily hopeful act, and I can't think of anything that makes me prouder of you."

"One foot in front of the other," says Oliver.

"Always. I'm here if you need anything. 'Kay?" She releases him from a hug. "Anything."

"Coming, Ollie?" Del asks, quick to make his way back to the other Manhunt players as Kirby and their aunt head upstairs. Del is expecting Oliver to follow.

But as soon as Chief Wachs is out of sight, Oliver falls behind. "Hey, I think I have to bail on Manhunt today," he calls out. "Sorry!"

"Seriously?" Del replies in frustration.

As Oliver turns away, he thinks about how his aunt found the energy to make more time with Kirby, even though she surely has a billion things she ought to be doing.

Oliver turns back to his best friend. "Hey, do you want to hang out later, though?"

Del doesn't answer right away. "Oliver . . ."

"I could come over and bring food from the dining hall if you want."

"Oliver—"

"Or whatever you want. Sorry."

"Ollie, I'm really trying to do well with Manhunt and the school placement tests and everything. I need to *work*."

"Okay, we'll study together, maybe?"

"Maybe," says Del, heading away with a wave. "Manhunt's going on 'til it's too dark to see, if you change your mind."

Oliver feels like he did something wrong, but he's not sure what.

He turns away, facing the official zombie brigade vehicle that his aunt drives. He goes to the trunk and discovers it's slightly ajar. *Uh-oh.*

Oliver's heart nearly explodes with the amount of adrenaline pumping through it.

He looks around in every direction for his escaped zombie prisoner. Quickly, he realizes he's out of practice with doing his safety-identification sweeps.

But just as the different parts of Oliver's brain all start coming up with contingency plans—call 9-6-6! No, call Aunt Carrie! Forget that, just walk away . . . keep going until no one knows your name!—

There's a low moan from the cracked-open trunk.

Cautious as he's ever been in his life, he goes to find a stick and uses that to ease the trunk wider and wider.

A zombie's eyes peer back.

With how weak the monster is, they're not glowing from the inside, but that makes them even more horrible, since they're red as dry blood—and the scent of iron and rotten eggs faintly tickles Oliver's nose.

The monster doesn't move as Oliver comes closer an inch at a time.

"I'm here to help, okay?" says Oliver experimentally. It feels incredibly strange.

There's no answer from Regina's supposedly smart zombie.

"Look," Oliver tries again, feeling even more uncomfortable. "If you really *can* talk, like Regina said, you should say so."

The zombie shifts to look past Oliver, searching the area. But that's all.

Oliver's doubts about this continue to grow.

"All right, look. We need to move quick now. If you make *any* trouble, you're getting soaked. End of story. Understand?"

Again, the zombie simply stares.

"Phoenix, right? That's your name? Nix for short?"

The zombie lowers his head slightly, still staring, eyes never blinking. Oliver's not sure if it's a nod or a warning.

"Okay, let's move. I've got to get you across campus and into the library while it's quiet."

Still, the zombie doesn't react.

Oliver thinks.

Keeping an eye on the car, he heads to a trash can and takes out the bag inside. He carries it back to the car.

He thinks very, very hard about what he's about to do.

Slowly, he extends a hand into the bag of trash. It's extremely gross, but he barely notices.

From the trash, he retrieves the end of a sandwich and offers it on his upturned palm. "I'm sorry I threatened you before. It wasn't nice. But Regina says you're smart. Why would we do all of this if we wanted to hurt you?"

Still nothing. Oliver is running out of ideas.

He throws down the garbage bag and rubs his eyes.

And he thinks hard, trying to understand.

What would it be like if *he* were a zombie being hauled to a strange place in a trunk? A zombie who could understand what was going on. *Does* he know what's going on?

"This is too much," Oliver says to himself.

He opens his eyes again and finds a nightmare face staring into his eyes. He shrieks, panicked.

Nix has stopped advancing, though. He's going through the trash bag Oliver dropped, eating everything he can grab. Shoving it into his horrible, yawning mouth. Eyes *locked* on Oliver.

As threatening as the look seems, it's clear that Nix would have already attacked Oliver if he intended to.

There's nothing to do but wait for him to finish, Oliver decides.

It's horrifying to witness—and to know that this monster has performed this act of devouring an uncountable number of times before. Worse, surely. Tearing apart the planet. Killing people, for all Oliver knows.

Rather than continue to think about this, Oliver uses the time to access his mental map of the campus, honed by his explorations and games of Manhunt. To his surprise, he realizes that there's a lot of detail in his head. He plots a route that avoids pathways and weaves through leaf-sheltered shortcuts, going well off the most direct route to pass the rear of buildings instead of the front.

But there's a problem: It's still bright daylight.

There's an obvious solution, of course.

It makes Oliver a little nauseated, though.

When Oliver looks back at Nix, there's no more trash to be seen. Even the bag is gone.

He watches Oliver, expectant.

"Ready now?" Oliver says. "Let's go, then."

Oliver can feel a small flare of heat now, coming from the zombie's direction. Nix's eyes are brighter orange again, if just barely.

There's never a circumstance when it's a good idea to turn your back on a zombie, Oliver decides, so they stay side by side as Oliver ferries a deadly threat through the unprotected campus, to a quiet spot in the mouth of a culvert that carries away stormwater. There's a trickle passing through it now, and Nix won't come any closer.

"We're going to have to hide out here for a while," says Oliver.

Darkness is still over an hour away, he knows.

Long time to sit and worry.

He looks at Nix.

"Why did I promise to keep you safe for *two days*?" Oliver says, reminding himself as much as he's informing Nix.

The seconds feel almost infinitely long.

"Two *days.*"

Nix barely seems to care at all. Which is probably for the best, Oliver decides. Tuning his keen observational skills in to the unmoving statue-like zombie, whose eyes are locked on the water trickling past them, Oliver gets a strange sense of purpose. He's not sure Regina is doing the smartest thing, but there *is* something about this zombie that triggers a curiosity inside Oliver. He's not exactly sure why. He's not exactly sure he *likes* it, either.

"Two days," Oliver says again, more determined.

He tries to engage Nix in conversation a few times, but despite Regina's insistence that he's communicated with her actually spoken to her in words—he shows no such ability to do so at all right now. Or no interest in doing so, at least.

And the time slowly passes, the Dusk-orange sky bringing a twilight eeriness for which Oliver has a newfound appreciation. The half-light will make it much harder to pick out Nix as a zombie. Oliver checks in with

Kirby and updates her on the situation. With the Manhunt game still going on, Oliver hasn't been missed at home, but he'll have to show his face pretty soon and swap places with Kirby.

With a heavy sigh, Oliver decides there'll never be a better time than now to make a move.

"All right. This is it," Oliver says. "Act alive, pal."

Nix blinks silently.

"Okay, fine, it was a terrible joke. But seriously, try to blend in. Gets tricky from here. And if we get caught, I don't know what happens to me, but we both know what happens to *you*."

Getting through the campus goes mostly smoothly, to Oliver's relief. He retreats to the shadowy areas twice when he sees people walking nearby, but nobody expects to see a zombie acting like a person, so nobody gives Nix and Oliver a second glance.

Getting into the library is a different story. This was always going to be rough . . .

"It's just like Manhunt, Ollie," he tells himself, staring at the giant concrete building. "You just need to avoid getting spotted, that's all."

He looks at Nix uncertainly.

"You ever play Manhunt with the other kids when you were alive?" Oliver asks.

For the first time, he senses a flare of that awful hunger all zombies possess—

Not the sort of hunger that makes Oliver reach for a superchiller to extinguish the threat, though. This hunger is . . . a loneliness that cuts Oliver like a knife: Nix doesn't have *anyone*.

Now's not the time to worry about that, Ollie, he thinks.

"Okay, Nix," says Oliver. "You just stay with me. Got it?"

Oliver's heart thumps hard as he does the unthinkable . . . he turns his back on Nix, poring over the situation ahead of him with all his years of Manhunt experience.

As he heads for the door, he suddenly realizes that his skills aren't exactly what he remembers . . . his thoughts are more muddled, his steps less sure-footed.

"Oh my gosh!" he hears a girl's voice call out.

We're made! Oliver thinks, suddenly envisioning the worst. But then he turns—

Oliver sees his sister.

"Kirby?" he whispers.

Kirby isn't paying attention to Oliver. All her attention is fixed on the zombie. "It's *you*," she says.

Nix is equally focused on Kirby, Oliver realizes.

"Kirby, wait. You two know each other?"

Kirby turns to Oliver. "You don't even recognize him."

Oliver turns back to squint at Nix. "What are you talking about?"

Kirby focuses on Oliver. "Ollie." She rolls up her sleeve and shows Oliver the mark on her arm.

Suddenly, a memory clicks into place.

Oliver looks at Nix with fresh recognition as Kirby continues:

"He saved your *life*, Oliver. That day in Redwood, in the minivan with Mom and Dad and Del? After the storm. After all the flooding. There were the zombies in the water, hunting us, and there was that one *other* zombie who *helped* us? Don't you recognize him? Or did you get him mixed up with all those many, many *other* helpful zombies you've met?"

Oliver remembers.

Still, Kirby continues: "That zombie saved our whole family, and Del, too. He jumped into the water and fought them and—look, I don't know what happened, but one minute it was certain death for us and then the next minute it *wasn't*, and he's the reason why."

"We can't talk about this out here, Kirby."

Kirby nods.

"Once we're in the basement no one will bother us. But we need to make it through a big open main area unnoticed first. Kirby, you can make a scene, right? Something to get everyone watching you?"

"Ha ha," says Kirby. "I *could*, sure. *Or* we could just go in the staff entrance, which leads right into the back of the stacks."

Kirby drops something from her hand. It dangles on a lanyard.

"Mom's ID badge?" says Oliver.

"Borrowed it. Don't tell her."

Oliver notices Nix's head swivel to look at Kirby. He thinks he can detect Nix's horrible face faintly grinning.

13

THE GREATEST SHOW ON EARTH

Joule Artis moved to New York to get away from zombie season.

It was supposed to mean a new start for her and her mother after they lost Joule's father in a flashpoint.

But then there was the monster in the belly of the whale.

"Trojan Corpse," the local newspaper has been calling it, to her mother's extreme irritation. And even though they survived by racing across the beach to the ferry, Joule could sense that her mother's dream of safety for her family was shattered for good.

It's becoming all too clear that, wherever we live, I can't protect you from the zombies, Joule, her mother said. *All I can do is . . . all I can do is prepare you. This trip, it's about giving you the best chance in this world.*

What trip? Joule asked.

". . . And then a week later, here I am back in California, on my way to be part of a research expedition that your dad and my mom set up," Joule tells Regina.

She's still shaken up from relaying the whole story of the zombie attack to Regina. How the surfers had lost their lives, punished for trying to rescue a helpless whale. How the cars were trapped in a traffic jam that made them easy prey for the surging zombie as it came ashore. How Joule and her mother only avoided the same fate because they ran to the ferry and escaped the blocked road.

"Yeah. So. I'm a big fan of public transportation now," says Joule. "Ferry boats specifically."

She pats the railing of the ferry boat on which she and Regina stand as it crosses the bay toward the San Francisco waterfront.

"I'm glad you're back, Joule," says Regina. "I know it's only a stop for the night, but it feels right with you here."

"I'm always here with you in spirit," Joule tells her with a grin. "But I *am* relieved to hear you trusted Ollie to help with the rebellion you're starting."

The world isn't ready for Regina Herrera and Ollie Wachs teaming up again, Joule thinks.

"Did I tell you he wants to bring in other kids to help, too?" asks Regina with frustration.

"Really? Great!" says Joule.

"Maybe," says Regina. "But it's dangerous. All it takes is trusting *one* wrong person to ruin everything. And then Nix gets extinguished, and HumaniTeam keeps going with its lies, and zombies become totally invincible."

"Okay," says Joule. "Although if you *don't* trust people, then all of those things are *definitely* going to happen. Because you can't do this all alone, and you know it."

"But—"

"No buts." Joule cuts Regina off. "You need all the friends you can get. Don't argue with me."

Regina lets out a moan of frustration. "I'm trying, Joule."

"Believe in your friends, Regina. We won't let you down."

"What about Kai?" Regina asks. "Of all the people I could've trusted, I shouldn't have trusted him, and it's lucky he didn't spark a whole new wave with his rebuilt NRG prototype. Not everyone's as good at making friends as you, you know."

Joule doesn't know what to say to this, other than the truth. "You're a human being, Regina. You're doing the best you can. Everyone makes mistakes. My dad always said the best way to make friends is to treat others how you want to be treated, and I think you're doing that," Joule says encouragingly.

"But what if how I want to be treated is for everyone to leave me *alone*?"

"Everyone? You want *everyone* to leave you alone?"

Regina frowns. "Not *you*."

Joule elbows her as the ferry boat eases into its mooring along the piers. "You're doing great, Regina."

"If you say so."

"I *do* say so."

As Joule and Regina observe, other passengers line up to be the first ones off the boat. Many of them look at their watches and phones in frustration, like they're late for something. It's like a bus station, but with a clean ocean breeze. Also, there's the calming rocking motion of the waves the whole time. And everywhere you look, on a rock or a pier, there's an adorable sea lion sunning itself.

It's much better than a bus station, Joule decides.

"Come on, you two," says Regina's father. "Late for launch."

"Lunch?" says Joule. "We already ate."

Mr. Herrera grins. "Launch, not lunch, Joule. Hurry up, you'll see."

As he hustles Joule and his daughter forward, he lifts Joule's large duffel bag off the deck and heaves it across his shoulders. They follow the crowd from the boat into the ferry terminal building, and as they do, there's a chain of booming sounds in the distance, like fireworks.

"Inside, everybody!" says the ferry attendant, holding a door open for the passengers.

The afternoon sky darkens rapidly, turning San Francisco Bay stormy green. Thunder rumbles in the distance.

Mr. Herrera allows Joule to puzzle out what's happening, and as the look of surprise registers in her eyes, he nods.

"*Launch*," says Joule. "As in . . ."

"Cloudbuster o'clock," says Mr. Herrera with a grin.

"But where are the sirens?" Joule asks. "Where's the Dusk Alert?"

"Things are different with the Cloudbusters," Regina explains to Joule. "HumaniTeam and the government have a partnership now. A contract that requires HumaniTeam to protect us—"

"A *covenant*, Gina," says Mr. Herrera, acting very relaxed about all of this.

Regina rolls her eyes. "They insist on calling it that. *The covenant.* It's just a fancy word for contract, though."

"Sky Stone has always been a showman. His hero is P. T. Barnum. You know who P. T. Barnum was, Joule?" asks Regina's father.

"No," says Joule.

"Oh, well! This is cool—"

"It's not cool," Regina whispers to Joule, loudly enough to be sure her father can overhear.

About then is when the sky tears open and torrents of rain and hail turn the landscape an opaque, dirty gray.

"P. T. Barnum was a huckster," says Mr. Herrera.

"What's a huckster?" asks Joule.

"Doesn't matter," Regina replies instantly.

"A showman," says Mr. Herrera. "Someone who can make people excited about what they're promoting. Which is what *this* exercise is all about. Making HumaniTeam look good, so they can make lots of money."

Joule watches the other onlookers, who are in a state of wonder and fascination at the storm's ferocity.

"Gather round, folks," says Regina's father. "HumaniTeam and Sky Stone are here to bring you the Greatest Show on Earth. Man's triumph over nature, mastery of the elements . . . vanquishing death itself!"

As if in response, the rain and hail stop like a faucet has been shut off.

"All right, show's over," says the ferry attendant to the gathered audience. "Move along, we've all got places to be."

"I don't understand," says Joule. "That was just . . . for show? There was no zombie flashpoint?"

"It's to *prevent* flashpoints, they say," Regina replies. "HumaniTeam's covenant with the city is that they'll keep the zombies from returning by suppressing them. Launching Cloudbusters every day during all of zombie season."

"*Every* day?"

Suddenly, Joule remembers how her flight had to abort its approach and circle for a couple of minutes before landing yesterday. How they had a little turbulence on the way to the ground, and afterward the captain apologized, "Sorry for the bumpy ride, but small price to pay for what we get in return, right?"

Joule didn't understand what that meant then, but now that she thinks about it, the time was probably exactly 3:45 p.m., just like today.

"That's a *lot* of Cloudbusters," says Joule nervously as they head out of the ferry terminal. She's seen firsthand what these weapons can do. What damage they really cause.

In Redwood, when the Cloudbusters were first tested, Joule saw this transformation happen before her eyes: A zombie that was struck by the supercooled water rose again, energized and immune to the icy blasts. An amphibious, swollen mutation that nearly tore her mother away from her, like Joule's father already had been.

But the people of Redwood all pulled together to save lives in the end, and that's exactly what Regina is trying to do now. What *everyone* should be doing now, Joule knows: finding ways to work together. Again and again. If humanity is to survive in a zombie-filled world, it'll take the whole planet working as a team.

And deep down, Joule thinks Regina knows it.

Regina's going to need more friends than she believes she does. A *lot* more.

She considers how to help with this, and has the beginning of an idea.

Outside the building, there's a huge farmers market that's returning to full swing—produce and prepared foods being swiftly fetched from the backs of vans, where they had been kept safe through the storm. Regina's father gets them all the most perfect-looking peaches Joule has ever seen.

It reminds her of the Santifers . . . and that reminds her of her father . . . and all the grief and loss hits her again.

As great as it is to see Regina, being back here isn't easy for Joule.

"Come on, Joule, can't miss your check-in," says Mr. Herrera, leading the girls down the pedestrian walkway along the bay, which connects all the piers. "I can't wait for you to meet my old pal Hugo Halyard! Your new teacher, too, I guess. What luck that I could match you two up on such short notice. Can't teach good timing, you know."

As they move, Joule notices all the sea lions resurfacing from their underwater refuge now that the storm has passed. They're pretty used to the Cloudbusters, it's clear.

Joule and Regina walk a few steps behind Mr. Herrera.

"Hey," says Joule. "I just got an idea."

"What's that?" Regina asks.

"I'm about to go meet a literal boatload of really smart kids our age. What if I did some recruiting for Team Regina? How does that sound?"

Regina looks suspicious. "What exactly would the point of that be?"

"Look," says Joule. "Oliver Wachs is right, Regina. You need more friends."

"Joule . . . thanks, but—"

"Think, Regina. You're trying to destroy HumaniTeam. You know how big a mission that is. You need help."

"I need *your* help."

"I *am* helping," says Joule. "This is me helping. By making sure that you're surrounded by people you can depend on. People who you can trust."

"Strangers?" says Regina.

"I was a stranger once, too," says Joule. "Think of them as little me's, okay? Just imagine them all with my face, but really annoying high-pitched voices."

"Little mini-Joules?" says Regina with a half-amused smile.

"Just think about it, Regina," says Joule.

"I'll think about it," says Regina, without meeting Joule's eye. And as she searches for a place for her eyes to rest, she says, "Hey! Look, Joule, we're here!"

As Regina points, Joule frowns, not letting herself be distracted from their conversation by the sight before her. Not by the giant WELCOME, STUDENT EXPLORERS! banner over the gangway leading up to the deck. Not by the other kids sizing her up, kids who she'll be spending the next month living and working alongside. Not even by the two different high-tech deep-sea mini-submarines suspended over the deck with a crane arm, or the frazzled man in blue coveralls bellowing instructions about taking better care of his babies.

Okay, fine.

Joule is quite distracted.

She senses Regina pause beside her as Mr. Herrera continues onto the deck of the ship, where he has already attracted the attention of a shaved-bald older man, also in blue coveralls, with a very straight back and a serious but cheerful demeanor.

"Hugo!" calls out Mr. Herrera.

The man laughs in surprise and takes three precise steps to close the gap with Mr. Herrera and shake his hand, pumping it up and down. "Mr. Herrera!" he says with a warm, fierce charm. "You're bringing me some new talent, I understand?"

"Professor Halyard is a wonderful friend of mine, we've known each other a long time," says Mr. Herrera as Joule and Regina climb aboard. Joule already knows this, though. Mr. Herrera's friendship with Hugo Halyard is the whole reason why Joule got the invitation to be a part of this expedition.

As Professor Halyard shakes Joule's hand, she instantly feels like she's one of the creatures under Professor Halyard's microscope. Not in a bad way—but definitely in a being-carefully-studied way.

She looks to Regina for some help, and Regina pulls Joule forward. "Let's go find the bunks?" she suggests.

Joule nods enthusiastically.

Belowdecks, Joule meets her two new counselors, Julua Fazekas and Agatha Dean, who are research assistants working on Halyard's team. She also meets the boys' counselor, a giant man named Guz Griffin, who peers down from an imposing face—heavy glasses sliding down a broken-looking nose, and a giant, stiff beard with streaks of white.

The other kids are all trying to sort out where they belong as well, and though most of them are a little bit on the quiet side, Joule gets a really warm and happy feeling about them. From the quick hellos with the seven other girls she's bunking with, she can tell that everyone's as excited to be here as she is. It fills her with a cautious hope, and a sense of purpose.

Joule turns to Regina. "Come on, let's go meet the others and get off on the right foot."

"Do I have to?" says Regina.

Joule nods. "A good leader has to connect with their teammates, Regina."

"Don't tell them anything about you know what!" Regina whispers.

"Promise," says Joule. "Not until you give the okay."

Across the bunks, Joule spies a quiet girl named Katrina, who smiles at Regina and Joule. Joule is about to go over and say hi when there's a commotion up on deck. Everyone pours out of the cabin and climbs up the steps to see what's afoot.

Joule sees a helicopter on the deck of the ship. Blades still spinning, with a HumaniTeam logo on the side.

Joule feels the waves of tension coming off Regina and turns to see her friend scowling. "Crap," says Regina. "Sky."

"What?" Joule can barely make out her voice over the sound of the helicopter.

"*Sky,*" Regina repeats darkly.

"The sky?" Joule says, looking around wildly. Thinking it's another hailstorm.

But Regina's eyes are locked on the passengers stepping out of the aircraft—a man, a woman, and two boys. She glares hardest at the man, who walks across the ship like he owns the world. As if feeling her angry glare, the man turns and recognizes Regina.

"Gina!" he says with a wolfish grin.

"Hello, Mr. Stone," says Regina, unsmiling.

"I'm Sky," says the man, introducing himself to Joule before returning his gaze to Regina. "An unexpected pleasure to see you," he says. "Hang around for me, maybe? I gotta do my thing here, but then I'd love to take you and your dad wherever you're going in the whirligig." He arcs his thumb toward the helicopter.

The man doesn't wait for an answer before he heads away, pulling the attention of everyone else on the ship in his wake, like the sun pulls planets into their proper orbits. "Everybody? I just wanted to drop in to say bon voyage, and thank you for your dedication to studying this precious world of ours. You're gonna need everyone working together if you're going to save Planet Earth."

"I hate him so much," says Regina.

Joule gives Regina a pointed look. "Then let's show these kids what a real leader looks like."

"Fine," Regina agrees. "If you find people here you can trust, then I will, too. *But*. You see this kid coming up to us right now?"

Joule follows Regina's gaze and sees a boy with red hair and pale, freckled skin approaching. He's one of the boys who got off the helicopter.

"Do *not* trust him," says Regina. "That's Kai Stone."

"Kai?" says Joule. "As in your friend Kai?"

"Yep."

"So the guy you're fighting to destroy . . . is your family friend?"

"It explains a lot about why I'm like this, right?"

Before Joule can reply, Kai arrives.

"Regina?" calls Kai. "What're you doing here?"

"I'm here to drop Joule off," Regina answers.

"Hi," says Joule.

"This is the famous Joule?" Kai says. He gets a broad, plastic smile on his face that clearly marks him as Sky Stone's offspring and makes a tiny bow in Joule's direction. "I've heard all about you from Regina. Are you on this expedition, too?"

"I am," says Joule.

"Great!" says Kai. "Any friend of Regina's is a friend of mine."

"What's going on over there?" Regina asks Kai, nodding toward the other two passengers. One is a woman standing apart from everyone else, eyeing them all like they are potential threats, and the other is a boy their age, who fiddles his fingers nervously.

"The kid? That's nobody," Kai says, without caring whether the boy hears the dismissal in his voice. Then he nods to the woman. "And Vic. You know Vic," Kai says.

"I don't, actually," says Regina.

"You don't know Vic Pinkerton? She's been my dad's number two awhile. But mainly they've been working up in Alaska."

As Joule watches, Vic Pinkerton supervises a set of giant equipment cases that are being unloaded and ferried quickly from the aircraft to somewhere belowdecks.

"What're those boxes?" asks Regina.

"That is top secret," says Kai with a mischievous grin. "If you find out, tell me, okay? I'd like to know, too."

As Kai carries his bags downstairs, Regina grabs Joule's arm, nails digging into the skin. "Watch him like a hawk, Joule."

Joule nods, and turns her attention to the other boy who arrived with Kai. A bewildered-looking boy still standing awkwardly beside the helicopter.

"Hey!" Joule calls out. "Are you part of this expedition?"

He nods awkwardly and replies, "Yeah, you?"

"Yeah. I'm Joule."

"Hey," he says. "I'm Anton."

14

SEA CHANGE

Anton Zarkovsky hadn't stepped on a boat in months before arriving on the *Undercurrent*, but the familiar movement of the ocean rocking the deck beneath his feet makes him feel more on balance, somehow. This is right where he's supposed to be, Anton's gut is telling him. It's what Alek would be doing if he were the one who'd survived.

"Next stop, trashapalooza!" calls out Professor Halyard excitedly, referring to the subject of their expedition—the Great Pacific Garbage Patch.

"I wish I was as excited about *anything* as that guy's excited about garbage," says Anton, mostly to himself.

The comment gets a laugh he wasn't expecting, and Anton looks around to see where it came from—instantly suspicious that *he's* the butt of the joke. But his suspicions evaporate when he sees it's the friendly girl who introduced herself before—*Joule*, he reminds himself.

He gets a little flustered at the attention anyway. He's much more comfortable being ignored.

Luckily, like everyone else on the ship, Joule's eyes are drawn up to the bright orange structure looming over them. The Golden Gate Bridge. They all crane their necks to look up at one of civilization's modern wonders as the boat churns through the water.

"Never seen the bridge from down here," says Joule.

"I've only seen it in pictures," says Anton awkwardly.

Joule nods politely. Her attention is already beginning to drift.

He sneaks a self-conscious glance at Joule, not sure what to make of this extremely tall Black girl in her oversized canvas jacket and hiking boots, who was curious to meet him and who laughed at his joke. But what he is sure of is that he doesn't want their conversation to end quite yet.

"D-do you like bridges?" Anton asks.

What kind of question is that, Anton? he asks himself.

"I mean. Who doesn't?" says Joule.

"Not me!" Anton says, embarrassed at his eagerness. "Um, I mean, I think they're cool, too. Not as cool as trash islands, obviously."

"Obviously," Joule agrees, laughing once more. "Speaking of trash islands, how did you end up here on this expedition?"

As Anton starts to answer, he suddenly realizes he can't tell her the real answer. He'd be breaking a promise. He'd be betraying Sky and all the hardworking HumaniTeam employees back in Munivit.

We're going to save the world, Anton, but our work cannot proceed without secrecy was what Sky told Anton and his father. *There are enemies out there just as dangerous as zombies are, and far more clever. Spies from our rivals trying to steal our designs, government officials slowing down everything without a care*

for the cost, and perhaps worst of all, even within HumaniTeam itself, there are
those who want to stop all of this.

To put it more simply, the fate of the zombiefighting tool of the future rests in Anton's hands. If he spills the beans, Sky's foes will win. And that means Anton—and Anton's whole family, who are moving up in the world thanks to Sky's generosity, with high-paying work, with opportunities to get fancy educations—will lose.

Anton's eyes flit across the deck, to Vic Pinkerton, who has a deep crease of impatience on her forehead. She sees Anton looking at her and stares back with an intensity that reminds him of watching her subdue that giant zombie in Munivit Bay. Even if Anton's deleted all the videos, as he promised to do—even if he'll never speak a word about the heroic deeds he saw—he can still picture it perfectly in his mind. That can never be erased.

And he suspects that he has a very good guess about what's in the top secret crates she brought with her here onto the *Undercurrent* . . . the weapon that she used in Munivit to incapacitate the monster: the Eel. Whatever she's doing with it here must be very important.

When Anton glances back at Joule again, she's got an unhappy expression on her face.

"That lady gives me the creeps," Joule confesses.

"Vic? She's awesome," says Anton. "She gets things done. She—"

Anton barely stops himself once again.

"She what?" asks Joule.

"She's, like, Sky Stone's apprentice," Anton says, avoiding once more any mention of HumaniTeam's secret project. "And the reason I'm here is because I want her job one day."

Joule looks like she's curious to hear more, but then she lets it go. "Good luck," she says.

"What about you?" he asks Joule.

"How'd I get picked for this? You remember my friend who came here with me today? Regina?"

"Yeah?" says Anton.

"Well. She's why I'm here. Or, her parents are. The Herreras have worked for HumaniTeam for a long time, and her dad knows Professor Halyard from a project they both worked on together long ago . . ."

"Ah," says Anton. He shrugs like he doesn't care, but he's actually paying extremely careful attention. The name Herrera triggers a warning in his brain: Dr. Celeste Herrera is well-known to everyone working with Sky Stone in Munivit—she's one of the Cloudbuster's enemies within HumaniTeam itself. She's been out to destroy the whole project since the start. *Is it possible Joule is part of all that, too?* he wonders.

"So you live around here?" Anton asks, shaking off his suspicion.

"Used to. Grew up here. But after the Rogue Wave, me and my mom moved to New York."

She seems hesitant to say more.

Anton nods. Everyone's heard about the disastrous Rogue Wave that turned this whole part of California upside down, and introduced the world to the miraculous Cloudbuster.

Joule presses on. "Now we're leaving *there*, too, maybe? I don't know. The whole point of going was that it was supposed to be a place that'd be safer. Where it rains more, and the zombies can't get to you with all the water. Except . . . except the water is actually dangerous, too, these days."

Anton reflexively flinches away as her words summon the memory of a giant, algae-slick zombie, reaching with slimy boulder fingers.

She notices it, and Anton notices her noticing.

"You've seen something, too?" she asks.

He swallows hard. "Uh-huh."

She waits, giving him space to keep going. He can't talk about the incident he recorded, he knows. But he wants to share *something*.

"One of them wrecked my family's fishing boat," he says, feeling the cards in his pocket. He tells her about how it ate all the fish in the net, and that made it get bigger. He doesn't mention Alek at all. He doesn't mention Sky or Vic or Munivit.

"Anton, that's awful," she says. "I'm so sorry."

He just shrugs and looks away, attempting to hide the half-truth.

"Anyway," says Anton. "What did *you* see?"

Joule stiffens, clearly not wanting to talk about it, but pushes through the feeling and tells him, "I saw one come onto land. At the beach. I was . . . I was right there, when . . ."

Joule trails off.

"You don't have to say," Anton tells her gently. "I know what it's like."

"Fair enough. Seen one giant invincible zombie, seen 'em all. Right, Anton?" she jokes.

He shrugs. "I prefer the term 'abominable no-man.'"

Joule doesn't laugh at the joke.

"Wow, not even a courtesy laugh," Anton remarks.

"What?" says Joule. "Oh. Good one. Sorry," she says. She looks out at the fog. "It's just—I'm just thinking. You and I both saw them with our own eyes, right?"

Anton nods.

"It's just . . . I don't know. It kinda makes me wonder . . . are we too late already?"

"What do you mean? Too late for what?"

"Can I tell you something, Anton?" says Joule.

He nods again.

"I'm pretty sure we're not on this expedition because Professor Halyard is interested in trash, actually. I'm pretty sure he's interested in trash because *zombies* are interested in trash. At least, on land they are. It's a powerful zombie lure . . . and I'm betting that an entire *island* made out of it is gonna be like finding the lost island of Zombie Atlantis."

Anton stares at her. "You're telling me we're *trying* to find those things?"

"Well, I for one am tired of waiting for zombies to find *me*. I want to know what's really going on out there, so maybe we can stop it before it's too late. But if we both saw them in two different oceans already . . ."

She looks a little seasick.

Anton doesn't fully understand why. "What?"

"Okay, here's the thing. The planet is mostly covered with water, right?" says Joule. "Seventy-one percent of the whole world."

"Sure."

"And the ocean's full of fish and giant squid and seaweed and about a billion other things. We can't really count them all. It's so much bigger than the 'civilized' world."

"And isn't that why we're here? To *explore*?"

Joule takes a slow breath in and out. "That's exactly my point. We have no idea what's down there. Think about it, Anton. If they're starting to come onto dry land to hunt, that means . . ."

Anton gets it. "It means that's where they can find things to eat. It means they've already . . . it means . . ."

Joule nods. "They've already devoured all the living things at the bottom of the ocean . . ."

Anton tenses. "You think that zombies already conquered the ocean?"

Joule doesn't respond.

"How could the zombies have taken over seventy-one percent of the planet, and nobody even noticed? There has to be another explanation."

Amidst Anton's panicked thoughts, he can see the hope draining out of Joule. He has only just met her, of course, but seeing her like this makes him extremely sad.

She shrinks back, away from him.

"I'm sorry, Anton, I need to . . ."

"Yeah, okay." He feels totally useless.

"Nice to meet you, Anton," she says. "I'm sorry."

She turns away and hurries belowdecks toward the girls' cabin.

Giving her some space, Anton slowly traces her path, toward the same set of rattling stairs, which lead to the boys' cabin as well. But he's interrupted before he reaches them.

"Hold on there, Zarkovsky," says Lieutenant Pinkerton. Her tone is so commanding that Anton doesn't even think about disobeying her.

"Yes, uh, Vi—Lieutenant?" says Anton, fumbling around awkwardly in his flustered state.

"Remember what you promised," says Pinkerton.

"I remember," Anton says as eager as he is nervous.

"Remember that if you break your promise, it'll be your family that pays for it," says Pinkerton. "Understand me?"

"Yes, ma'am." Anton nods again, a little more nervous than eager this time.

Anton is well aware of the generosity Sky Stone demonstrated toward his family. In fact, he's in awe of the opportunities that have arisen almost overnight for the Zarkovsky family, and for everyone in Munivit who helps make Project Dawn successful.

This is the genius of Sky Stone. It's his core talent. He's not an inventor— he doesn't come up with any big ideas—he's an implementer. He turns someone else's big idea into the world's reality. And as Sky Stone pioneers and perfects the mass production of HumaniTeam's Cloudbuster system, the number of rockets they can build keeps doubling and doubling and doubling again.

Mind-boggling changes are afoot—in Alaska and across the globe. An extraordinary spiderweb of industry that will turn the tide of human civilization's fight against the zombie hordes.

"How long until we can tell people about the Eel?" Anton asks Lieutenant Pinkerton, itching to share the good news with his new friend, Joule. Something to give her hope that better times are ahead.

"If this trip goes well, everyone will know about what we've been working on very soon," says Pinkerton.

"That's good," says Anton.

Pinkerton eyes Anton head to toe. "But if you want to help," she says, "I'm going to need an assistant on this trip. No one else can know. But Sky thinks you've got a good head on your shoulders."

Anton feels his shoulders lift. But he doesn't want to make Sky's son any more of an enemy, so he asks again to make sure: "You don't want Kai?"

"You're here because you wanted a future working with us one day, didn't you?"

Anton nods eagerly. "Yes."

"Good, then. This is an opportunity to distinguish yourself."

"Aye aye, Lieutenant," Anton tells her. "Thank you."

He feels a slight rush of adrenaline as he remembers seeing Pinkerton stop a zombie surge single-handedly with the machine she calls *the Eel*—a Taser-like device that can deliver a shock as powerful as lightning. A tool that can stop the newest and most terrifying evolution of the zombie threat.

He can't wait to find out what she's *really* here to do.

15

SKY STONE

Regina is the first one out when the helicopter lands on the east side of San Francisco Bay, just down the road from the Herreras' new home.

"Thanks, Sky!" Regina calls out, extremely eager to get away from their host's hospitality. Or, more precisely: out of his *control*, which is *disguised* as hospitality.

"We can probably walk from here, Dad!" Regina suggests, not waiting for her father to answer as she starts away across the concrete helicopter-landing pad.

"In *this* heat? No way," Sky disagrees. "Get in, I'll just drive you the rest of the way."

"Thanks, Sky, that's very thoughtful," says Regina's father. "But only on the condition that you stay for dinner."

Sky gives them a dazzling white smile. "Deal."

"Greaaat!" says Regina, with the fakest fake enthusiasm in recorded history. She's finally mustered the courage to talk to her mother about Nix and her plan to tell the world about Project Phoenix, but that obviously can't happen while Sky is around.

Sourly, Regina climbs into the back seat of the chauffeured car that's waiting for Sky at the heliport and slams the door.

Regina stews in silence, fantasizing about the disgrace of Sky Stone.

She watches him approach the car and get in, talking to Regina's father like they're not enemies. *Sky wouldn't be this friendly if he didn't want something*, Regina reasons to herself. *But what's changed? What do the Herreras have that he wants?*

Watching and wondering, Regina is even more grateful that Joule is keeping an eye on Kai.

As they drive home, the itchy questions leave Regina feeling like she's about to crawl out of her skin, but Sky is seemingly in no particular rush. He'd be comfortable anywhere, really—and that is *not* a compliment.

Regina plays her fantasy all out in her head. The conversation with her mother where Regina announces the big news: *I've got proof that HumaniTeam is as rotten as any zombie ever was. That Project Phoenix is real. That they made smart zombies.* Flash forward to the press conference with a thousand reporters watching as the Herreras unveil Nix to the world, proof of the truth behind Regina's accusations. Smash cut to the shocked world demanding answers about the unthinkable experiment. A montage, maybe . . . Sky Stone being arrested and led off in handcuffs, that sort of thing . . . the Herrera name restored to honor, for outstanding contributions to the planet.

And then . . . ? It gets foggy from there.

Destroying Sky Stone won't solve the problems people are facing. That's a problem for another day, though. For right now, the satisfaction of punishing Sky for one of his many, many crimes is enough, she decides, as they arrive at the Herreras' home.

"Celeste!" says Sky, pulling Regina's mother in for a hug when she comes to the door in surprise.

"Been awhile, Sky," says Dr. Herrera as she disentangles herself as quickly as she can. "You're—?"

"—Staying for dinner," says Regina's father.

"Wonderfuuul!" says Regina's mother, establishing a new record for fake enthusiasm that will stand for a long time.

Mercifully, as soon as Regina's father retreats to the kitchen to start cooking, Sky turns to business . . . and wastes no time in getting to the point of why he's here:

"Celeste," he says to Regina's mother, "we need to fix this."

Dr. Herrera raises her eyebrows. "Fix what, exactly?"

"I want you to come back to work at HumaniTeam," says Sky. "So please. Stop giving us a hard time about the Cloudbusters. Humanity cannot afford to lose faith in our ability to fight the zombies."

She looks Sky straight in the eye. "You think it's better to lie and say everything is fine?"

"Everything *is* fine," Sky says, meeting her eyes unashamed. "People are living like normal again. It's safe for kids to play outside in the summer!"

"Sky . . . if this is why you're here, you're wasting both of our time."

She leaves him sitting there and heads into the kitchen to help cook dinner. "Let's hurry this up, Felix," she says to Regina's father.

Sky sits there patiently, as if he has all the time in the world.

"So, how's school?" he asks Regina.

"My school got destroyed by zombies, Sky," says Regina.

"Oh," he says. "Right."

"But I'm doing the homeschool thing with my dad. Learning a lot."

"That's lovely, Regina," he says insincerely.

"Yeah, thanks."

Then, ensuring Regina's parents are out of the room, Sky's voice gets quiet and he says, very calmly, "You need to give back what you stole, Regina."

"What?" Regina asks. She does her best to sound casual, but her heart is racing.

"What you scavenged from HumaniTeam's old Redwood office."

"I didn't *scavenge* anything!" Regina insists.

"Don't lie to me. I know you've been snooping where you don't belong."

Regina's puzzle brain clicks into gear: "*Kai* told you . . ."

"He told me everything. Project Phoenix?"

As soon as he says it, Regina's neck hairs stand on end.

Sky continues, "Out of respect for you and your family, I'm asking you nicely. Just once."

Regina keeps her face totally expressionless. "You know everything, then?" she says.

"Not everything. I don't know how you got company property out of Redwood, for one thing. That was very, very cleverly done. And I don't know where you've hidden the creature. But if you won't give it back willingly, I have to tell my people to find it. They're effective, I assure you, but they aren't very nice."

Regina stays silent, not giving in to panic or defeat.

He doesn't know where Nix is.

The game isn't over yet . . .

As the standoff continues, Regina's father calls out from the kitchen: "Dinnertime!"

"Have it your way," says Sky as he turns away, smiling a little too much.

"Well, at least you're taking me seriously now," Regina says, a bit more smugly than she'd intended.

"If what you want is to be taken seriously, Regina . . . you should take a cue from your mother and strike a deal with me," he says on the way to the dinner table.

Regina isn't sure what he means by this. It's not like her mother would ever go back to work for HumaniTeam—not after everything.

But it makes Regina desperate to talk to her mother and tell her the big news about Nix. She can't wait to show the world who Sky Stone really is and destroy him once and for all.

16

AT SEA

On the *Undercurrent*, there's a feeling of anticipation as the ship travels to the Great Pacific Garbage Patch, about halfway between Hawaii and California.

"Are you sure you're not worried, Mom?" Joule asks, speaking quietly into her headphone mic. She's sitting on her bed in the girls' bunk, using the unreliable satellite internet connection to call home.

"Do I look worried, honey?"

On Joule's phone, the grainy video stream shows Joule's mother smiling wide. On the stove behind her, there's a pot of lentil soup simmering.

"You look great, Mom."

"Are *you* worried, Joule?" her mother asks seriously.

Joule doesn't answer right away.

"That ship you're on is one of the safest places in the entire world, according to Professor Halyard," her mother continues. "Floating in the middle of the ocean, you should be safe from any zombie known to humanity."

"Unless they've learned to swim."

"Don't even joke," says Mrs. Artis.

"I know, Mom. I'm—I'm not . . . 'worried' isn't the right word."

There's a phrase Joule's heard people use before, but she never really understood what it meant. They'd say they were feeling "at sea." And now, Joule is beginning to understand that feeling herself.

It's the feeling of not being able to see land.

It's the feeling of drifting, not sure what you're moving toward. Not sure if you're even moving at all.

On the *Undercurrent*, Joule is very much "at sea."

Even with Kai to keep close watch on, and fourteen other potential new members of Team Regina to recruit, Joule can't help but feel terrified of the unknown underneath them here.

As Joule's silence lengthens, her mother seems to sense this complicated feeling, because she nods and says, "You're doing great, Joule. Trust your instincts. Trust yourself. You've been a student explorer for a very long time before they started calling you one. I wish your father could see you now."

"Thanks, Mom."

She's right, Joule knows. Her father would have been so excited to see Joule walking this path she's on—studying the world around her, discovering its secrets and working to protect them from harm. It's just . . . not easy living with such vast, shifting terrain right under your feet.

But Joule holds on to the good that her father breathed into the world and into her heart. She doesn't let herself give up.

Joule ends the call, then unlaces her hiking boots and kicks them off to let her feet breathe and relax. One of them tumbles off the edge of the bunk bed and crashes heavily on the deck below.

A tiny gasp comes from the bunk beneath her.

"Sorry, Katrina!" says Joule. "Sorry sorry—"

As Joule leans over the edge of the bunk, she sees Katrina with her noise-canceling headphones askew, playing bouncy pop music. "No worries!" says sweet, quiet Katrina in her Australian accent. "I wasn't asleep or anything. I was just surprised. Had music on, trying to not listen in on you."

"Thanks," says Joule.

"Go okay with the fam?"

"It was weirdly nice? My mom's being totally supportive and stuff."

"Is that *weird*?" asks Katrina.

Joule shrugs. "She worries. She's had a lot to deal with. Long story."

Katrina waits attentively.

"Moving to New York was supposed to mean she didn't have to worry about zombie season anymore. She could just be happy. But it didn't turn out that way." Joule considers telling Katrina everything. About losing her father a year ago, about Joule running away and scaring the heck out of everyone. About Joule's mother being attacked during a zombie surge—and then moving across the country only to have it happen all over again. Partially, Joule's decision to come on the expedition was because her mother had been kind of pushing her to.

She doesn't think her mother should be so hard on herself—especially after that day at the beach.

"You ever notice adults aren't doing that great these days?" says Joule.

Katrina nods. "Do they actually think they're fooling us?"

"Like we can't tell they're cracking up?" says Joule. "My mom made grilled cheese for dinner every day for a week before I left to come here."

"Oh man," says Katrina. "Why didn't you say something? We need to get you straight down to the mess, Joule."

"Is it lunchtime?" asks Joule.

"Let's go find out!"

"Sure."

"And then I want to ask Julia and Agatha Dean what the weirdest thing they've ever seen on a dive is."

"Good plan." Strangely, Katrina's warmth and friendliness make Joule's heart sit even heavier in her chest. Joule can't summon up any hope for their expedition right now—

That's what she couldn't tell her mother, she realizes.

In Joule's mind, it seems absolutely hopeless. There's nothing down there anymore except for zombies, she's half-convinced. And soon, the zombies' hunger will drive them toward land once more . . .

"Psst!"

As Joule startles and spins, Anton is there, gesturing for her to follow.

"Hey!" he says. "I was just coming to find you—look at this!"

Joule looks toward Katrina, who shrugs and starts to follow Anton.

"Are we allowed up here?" Joule asks as Anton ushers her and Katrina into a gallery that overlooks the nerve center of the *Undercurrent*.

"Nobody said we aren't. And I've been here for twenty minutes," Anton replies.

Below, there is a hive of activity. While the students have been busy exploring the ship, Professor Halyard has already gotten to work exploring the ocean deeps. A remote-operated deep-sea research sub called the *Fluke* is making its first dive.

Joule feels her curiosity return, pushing away all her worries, as the possibility of discovery comes into fresh focus . . .

And just for a moment, she thinks about how much her dad will be jealous he's not here.

But then Joule remembers that he's gone, that whatever's waiting at the bottom of the sea, she'll be dealing with it on her own.

17

RESPONSIBLE ADULTS

At the dinner table with her parents and their "friend" Sky Stone, Regina doesn't say a word for most of the meal.

It's all very "the adults are talking." So she just sits. Listening. Dreaming of horrible things happening to Sky—and Kai—Stone. In fact . . . while she's thinking about it, she texts Joule on the *Undercurrent*, asking if she could please push Kai overboard at the soonest moment possible.

"Put your phone away, Regina," says her father.

Regina pauses her text conversation with Joule, then slumps in her chair and listens.

"Come on, Celeste," Sky pleads again. "You want to make a positive impact on the world, right? Okay, well, just be honest: Are you going to achieve more by washing your hands of us and speaking out, or by doing the work you're *good at* and holding us to a higher standard from the inside?"

Dr. Herrera scowls. "That didn't work so great last time. I *kept* your secrets, like you pushed me to do. Even after I found out that you were hiding evidence that the superchillers were making the zombie problem *worse*—"

Sky interrupts her. "Superchillers are a safe, reliable tool and essential to the survival of our current way of life—"

Oh, gimme a break! Regina thinks. She *skreeks* her knife across her plate. Everyone turns.

"What about our future way of life, when superchiller-resistant zombies sweep across the world?" Regina asks.

Dr. Herrera's head turns to Sky, eyebrows lifted.

Regina feels her father gently nudging her, and she sees that she's balling her hand into a fist so tight that her knuckles are white.

"Sky," says Mr. Herrera. "More pasta?"

Regina counts to ten in her head, and starts to scheme about ways to tell the world what a creep Sky Stone really is. She imagines Nix in front of a camera. *I'm not the monster you should be scared of,* he's saying to the horrified masses. She imagines all the company's lies exposed. HumaniTeam in shambles.

"Sky," says Dr. Herrera, "when you talked to me about helping you with the Cloudbuster, you *promised* me that we wouldn't launch a single rocket unless the whole team agreed, together. And then you went back on that promise during the Rogue Wave."

"It saved your hometown, didn't it?" says Sky. "How many lives? Your daughter was there—"

"Yeah, I was there," Regina interrupts. "And I saw a zombie get blasted with a superchiller, and it only made the thing stronger."

"We believe it's a very small percentage of the horde. Less than one in a hundred."

"Okay, okay," says Regina. "So if there are a hundred billion zombies out there, that means we'll only end up with a billion of this new kind of zombie that is immune to our zombiefighting technology. Great work!"

Sky looks at Regina's mother thoughtfully but doesn't respond.

Dr. Herrera sighs and hunches over her plate. She's weakening, Regina notices with concern.

"It's complicated, I know," says Sky. "Regina's right. Cloudbusters have changed everything so quickly—given some of us the freedom to live normal lives, saved others from a terrible fate . . . but it comes with a cost. That's why I need you to put an end to this feud and come back to the pack. We're going to need you, for what's happening now."

"What's happening *now*?" asks Regina.

"We have to deal with the dead zones."

"Dead zones?" Regina repeats the unfamiliar phrase.

"It's a phenomenon that we've seen form in places like river deltas, where large numbers of the amphibious undead are swept out to sea. They feed and feed until there is nothing left. But very recently we discovered that there are dead zones in deeper waters, too. Places where we can't easily track their movement, or their size. But we know there's a giant one up in Alaska. And we're tracking it as it comes south, gathering strength off the coast."

"It's coming from Alaska?" Dr. Herrera asks. "What a coincidence that Alaska is home to your Cloudbuster manufacturing operation."

Sky brushes this aside. "There's no sense casting blame. We simply have to deal with it. Because if it comes ashore, our forecasters believe it could be an unthinkably destructive surge."

For a moment, the Herreras all sit in silence.

"What's your plan?" Regina's mother asks.

"I restarted an old project again," says Sky. "A tool we already have, fully developed and tested, just waiting to be deployed. It's proven *shockingly* effective against the amphibious undead. But this situation demands a more powerful version of the device. Which is why we need our best people. A united front. The only hope humanity has is if we all find *some* way to work together. *All* of us."

Regina's mother leans back in her chair and looks at Regina's father.

Regina's father thinks for a moment. Then he asks, "Which project is it you're restarting, Sky?"

"The Eel," says Sky.

"The *Eel*?" says Regina's mother. "That thing can hurt innocent people as easily as it stops a zombie."

"It's . . . a bit temperamental," Sky admits.

"You mean dangerous," says Regina's father. And then he adds: "Sky, on the *Undercurrent* today. What exactly was Vic Pinkerton doing there? Is she part of this?"

"Of course," Sky says. "When the US Air Force designs a new jet, they only entrust it to their most elite test pilots. She's our Air Force test pilot, for the Eel system."

Regina feels a jolt of worry. "I just sent my friend Joule out on that ship!"

"Don't worry, Gina," Sky says with that infuriating we-are-totally-pals tone. "They're safer on that ship than you and I are here. Why do you think I sent Kai out there? It's not because he's some great scientific wunderkind, I assure you. Don't worry about your friend. Worry about yourself. There's a dead zone coming our way, and when it moves onto land, it'll be unprecedented, I'm told . . . It's possible that everything near sea level within several miles of the shoreline would be consumed in moments."

Regina imagines the sight of an army of amphibious undead.

Thousands of zombies, each grown to the extraordinary size that things have a tendency to do in the vast darkness of the deep sea.

"It's *your* Cloudbusters that did this, Sky," says Dr. Herrera, breaking the silence. "You *have* to stop the launches . . ."

"We can argue about that later, when we have more time," says Sky. "Right now, dealing with the dead zone is all that matters."

A chill goes through Regina as Sky's intentions become terribly clear to her. "You don't even *want* to solve the zombie problem, do you?" she asks.

"I'm sorry?" says Sky. "What do you mean? I'm fighting them every day."

"That's exactly the problem!" says Regina. "Fighting them is all you care about . . . You want to go on and on fighting them forever. Making more and more money off more and more fighting."

As Regina speaks, Sky takes out his phone and reads a text.

"Now you're ignoring me?" says Regina.

Regina fixes Sky with a furious glare, but he simply acts like he can't hear her. Instead, he turns to Dr. Herrera. "Come back, Dr. Herrera. Please."

"You don't know that it's too late to fix the damage the Cloudbusters have done," says Dr. Herrera. "We need more information about what's really happening in the oceans right now."

Sky nods. "If you come back to work, you can work directly with Hugo Halyard to fix things, Celeste. But you keep saying you're not interested in that."

"After everything you've done, how can I possibly trust you, Sky?" asks Dr. Herrera.

"Why don't we do a little trial run right now?" Sky says. He lifts his phone and explains, "I've just received a request to launch a salvo of Cloudbuster rockets. Should we approve it? Or no?"

"You want my opinion?" Regina's mother says suspiciously.

"Well, why not? If you rejoin the company, it'd be *your* job to handle all of this, after all."

"What do you mean? Isn't that a big part of *your* job?"

Sky's eyes light up almost like they're zombie eyes in the darkness. "Dr. Herrera, I'm *offering* you my job."

"Huh," says Regina's dad. "And you would be . . . ?"

"I've been asked to step up and lead the whole company, starting immediately."

Once again, silence fills the room.

"We should probably deal with this immediately, Celeste. It's your friend Chief Wachs." Sky places his phone on the table so everyone can read it. "From Redwood. Simple 'approved' or 'denied' is all they need."

The Herreras all look at one another.

Then, as Dr. Herrera picks up the phone and calls Chief Wachs, clearly accepting her new assignment, Regina takes out her own phone and messages Joule about what she's just learned—about Kai's betrayal. About the dead zone. Most importantly? About the Eel.

There's a secret zombiefighting weapon being tested on the Undercurrent, she messages. *It's dangerous, Joule. Be careful.*

18

SHAKEDOWN

"We're descending through the water column," says Professor Halyard.

From the gallery that overlooks the nerve center of the *Undercurrent*, Joule watches the descent of the deep-sea research vessel called the *Fluke* alongside Katrina and Anton.

"The remotely operated vehicle is connected to the *Undercurrent* through a cable that carries signals up and down—allowing us to control it, and to see through its cameras as it gradually moves through the different, unique layers of the ocean," Halyard explains. "Closest to the surface and closest to land are the layers where the sun can reach, and these support the kinds of creatures we're used to seeing. But most of the ocean is alien to us. Deeper, beyond the twilight, the ecosystems are far more exotic— home of creatures that humans have rarely seen . . . if ever!"

A large monitor displays the data the submarine is transmitting back to the ship, from thousands of feet below the ocean's surface. There's also a video, but it only shows a headlamp shining on empty, dark water.

"This is fantastic," says Katrina, taking in everything around her. "Are we *really* allowed in here, Anton?"

"Just a shakedown dive today, folks," says Halyard's second-in-command, Dr. Aldo Aldi. It's only when Dr. Aldi turns and winks to the three student explorers above that they understand that they are very much allowed to be here. "A shakedown dive is a trial run, focused on getting everyone comfortable and detecting any problems with the new equipment."

"Why didn't they just say we should come watch?" Anton asks Joule and Katrina, slightly annoyed. "Why make it so complicated?"

As Joule considers this, she looks around at the gallery—it's set up as if the whole *point* is to watch and learn. Anyone paying attention should be able to puzzle that out.

"I think they want us to figure out *for ourselves* what we should be doing."

"What do you mean?" asks Katrina.

"I think they're teaching us how to be explorers right now," Joule explains. "And scientists, too," she adds. "Isn't this what Halyard and all the other people here do in their own work? Explore, and try to understand what's going on all around them? If they waited around for someone to tell them what to do, nothing new would ever be learned or discovered. It'd all be—"

Joule suddenly breaks off.

There's something on the video screen.

An octopus. Fleshy suction cups clinging to the lens and releasing, its parrotlike beak filling the frame. It pulls the camera to look into its eye, which looms huge on the vast monitor.

"Mina!" calls out Dr. Aldi. "Stop playing around, you're gonna break it."

The octopus, being both thousands of feet away and incapable of understanding human speech, does not stop playing around.

The video from the camera turns fuzzy and staticky as the octopus continues to play.

"Mina?" says Anton, looking at Joule and Katrina.

"Mina!" says Katrina.

Joule feels something awaken inside her. The hopelessness that she's gotten so accustomed to pressing down on her gives way to a gush of awe.

New friends, new opportunities, the octopus's playful curiosity—these are all living proof that the worst has *not* come to pass—and they fill Joule's lungs with something that feels lighter than air.

She feels a laugh bubble up inside her, but by the time it gets to her mouth, it sounds almost like a sob. She's not sad, though. It's the sound of sadness evaporating . . .

The octopus continues her exploration, riding the *Fluke* like it exists for her and her alone.

"I think she believes *she's* the one investigating *us*," says Joule.

Out here, the world seems both bigger and smaller at once. Like when Alice went down that rabbit hole and had to figure out the rules of Wonderland.

Joule looks from Anton to Katrina to the hardworking deep-sea explorers below, letting herself feel gloriously alive.

Then she feels a buzz in her pocket, and she takes out her phone to see that she's gotten several messages from Regina, each one more alarming than the last.

19

ROOM B4

Deep in the mazelike university library, Oliver and his sister have been watching Nix for over twenty-four hours, barricaded in the windowless, concrete-walled room B4. He and Kirby have been trading places through the day and night, and making excuses for why they're not where they *should* be.

It's an ideal place to stash a zombie for a couple of days. With the Stuxville University dorms all full of ZDPs instead of college students, the library is empty and quiet. Plus, Oliver's mom volunteers there, which means nobody thinks it's odd seeing the Wachs kids coming and going.

That doesn't mean Oliver feels comfortable with the situation, though. In fact, he's caught between exhaustion and panic. Despite Regina's reassurances, part of Oliver worries that Nix has just been waiting for his time to strike.

So when Oliver hears the sound of a latch going *click!* he gets jumpy and spins toward the zombie—

Nix is curled up with his back to the room. Perfectly still, only gentle moans proving that he's not fully extinguished.

Oliver breathes out, and turns to see Kirby closing the door behind her.

"Anything?" asks Kirby.

"Just some tiny moans. I think he might be hibernating. Like, he thinks he's buried underground. He's not that off base, actually."

Kirby frowns. "Oliver, don't get mad. I've been thinking . . ."

"You've been thinking about what?" Oliver asks wearily. The stress of the sleepless night has made his muscles ache.

"I've been thinking we should feed him again."

"We are *not* feeding him," Oliver says, absolutely firm. "I like him like this. I know he's not gonna go anywhere. And until Regina can get here with an exit strategy, I want him in hibernation."

"What if he's in pain or something?"

"Look, Kirby," Oliver says in his most big-brother voice. "Number one? Hibernation is how zombies spend about nine months of the year. Number two: The worst thing that can happen to him already happened to him. Y'know?"

"That's just another reason to be kind," says Kirby.

Oliver feels a rush of love for his sister. "Yeah. You're right. I think I'm just pretty tired."

"Go *sleep*," says Kirby.

He nods wearily and gets ready to leave. He hates leaving Kirby alone with the zombie, but they have a plan in place in case of emergency. The second it looks like the creature is waking up, she'll run out of the room, lock the door, and text Oliver.

"Ollie?" Kirby adds. "We can't keep staying here round the clock like this."

"We can't leave a zombie on the loose, unguarded, either."

"He's not our prisoner. We're *protecting* him."

Oliver sighs. "Same difference."

"No, Ollie. *Actual* difference." Before he can respond, both their phones suddenly erupt with the dreaded Dusk Alert sound.

DUSK ALERT: A flashpoint has been sighted in Redwood, California. The existing mandatory evacuation remains in effect until further notice. There will be no additional Cloudbuster launches at this time.

As Oliver reads the alert, he imagines Redwood falling to the horde.

Panicked thoughts brew in the back of his head, and Oliver tries to figure out what he can do to help. But the phone in his hand vibrates with an incoming call from Regina. He gestures for Kirby to come and listen, and answers it:

"Hey, Regina. Good timing!" he says, putting the call on speakerphone. "Did you just get a Dusk Alert about zombies in Redwood?"

"Yeah," Regina's voice comes through the speakerphone. "Ollie, listen—"

"Why does it say there's not going to be a Cloudbuster launch?" Oliver interrupts. "What's going on?"

"There's a lot going on right now, Ollie," says Regina. "It's bigger than Redwood. Everyone living in this whole part of California is about to be trapped between two hordes of zombies."

Oliver's stomach drops, like he's at the top of a roller coaster going into free fall. "*Two* hordes?" he says.

Across the room, Nix stirs. He seems to be coming awake from his hibernation, as if roused by the sound of Regina's voice. Oliver grabs Kirby's arm, ready to spring into action if anything goes wrong.

"One is the horde you already know about," says Regina. "And the other one . . . it's like the one you and I escaped from together. A whole zombie wave that's immune to superchillers and Cloudbusters—"

"Amphibious zombies?" Oliver asks, still eyeing Nix warily.

"It's called a dead zone," she explains.

Oliver's heart speeds up. "But . . . but they're supposed to stay in the ocean, aren't they?"

"They can't stay on land permanently, but they're coming ashore to feed now."

"You're sure?"

"Yes."

"Why is this happening?" Oliver asks.

"They're zombies, Ollie. They feed and feed until everything's gone. And if the oceans aren't enough for them anymore . . ."

"Yeah. Okay." Oliver feels the beginning of a familiar numbness. The old zombie season feeling. The panic of living in an unsafe world is back, worse than ever . . .

"How could people let this happen?" says Oliver.

"Not *people*," says Regina angrily. "*Person*. One person is responsible for all of this. Sky Stone. The new CEO of HumaniTeam. He wants this battle to go forever . . . which is why we're going to take him down."

"You want to . . . you want the two of us to take down the leader of HumaniTeam?"

"And Nix," says Regina. "You and me, and Nix. That's the whole point of protecting him. And it's why I'm calling. I'm coming to get him. I need to know where to meet you."

"Okay," says Oliver, then gives her directions to the library where they're hiding Nix. "Get here as soon as you can. But after that . . . I might have to go, okay?"

"Go?!" says Regina. "Go where? I thought we were a team."

"I *can't* lose Redwood," says Oliver quietly. "Not again."

Once more, Oliver imagines Redwood falling to the horde. Weirdly, it's the old version of the town he pictures, in his imagination. The one he remembers and loves. Not the soulless place it is becoming now. He ignores this tiny little detail and presses onward:

"I'm gonna call my aunt. Maybe I can find a way to help her fight the horde. Maybe those tunnels we were mapping . . ."

Regina pleads with him to reconsider. "Ollie, you can't leave . . . I can't do this without you. Will you just trust me? Help me, *one* more time?"

"I do trust you, Regina, but . . . but, like . . . if I asked you to help me— if I told you destroying Sky Stone isn't as important right now as saving Redwood, would *you* drop everything for *me*?"

Regina is silent for a moment.

"Is that what you really want, Ollie?" she asks.

In his head, the sudden numbness fills every crack like cement. "Yes, Regina," he says. "Getting back to normal . . . that's all I want."

"Okay, Oliver," says Regina. "Put me on video. I need to talk to Nix."

As Oliver turns to Nix, expecting to see him curled into a ball, he finds the zombie sitting up, watching Oliver with silent curiosity. Like any human might, if they knew they were being talked about.

20

STAY

"Can you see us, Regina?" Oliver asks, pointing his phone camera at Nix. Regina recognizes the face that she still sees in her nightmares. She'll never admit it to anyone alive, but Nix scares her more than anything else. More than death. More than mediocrity.

She's scared of ending up like him. In a prison between humanity and monstrosity . . .

She will never forget how Nix told Regina that she and he were alike. How he demanded that she stay and join him, half human, half monster, as leaders of the horde . . . and how Regina could feel her humanity slipping away. How a hunger filled her—

No one knows why some people return as zombies and others don't. But Regina's terrifying experience with Nix lingers in her mind. The bottomless need—the hunger for more that consumed her wasn't something that infected her from Nix's touch. It's something that she recognizes inside her, even now, in this call with Oliver. Regina believes very strongly that her choices in life will determine whether she ends up among those who lose their humanity and become zombies in death.

But she puts that all to the side and focuses on the problem before her. She looks Nix in his unsettling orange eyes.

"Hello, Nix," says Regina.

He says nothing, but his eyes remain fixed on hers. The connection between them she once felt is still there.

In her head she's practiced what she'd say to him the next time they were face-to-face. She has a whole speech about how she can't forgive him for the truly monstrous things he did back in Redwood . . . how he hunted her and attempted to kidnap her . . . taking her back to the horde by force. Because in his twisted mind, he thought that was how to make friends.

They are never going to be friends.

But in the light, Regina discovers that his red-orange eyes aren't quite as zombielike as she remembers them in her nightmares. There's something slightly deeper in them than before, she notes with a sudden curiosity.

The whole speech evaporates.

"Okay," Regina says into the phone. "First things first: I'm on my way to get you, Nix. But before that? We need you to do something for us. To start making up for some of the damage you've done."

He waits, an attentive look on his face.

"I want you to take command of the zombies that are massing in Redwood, but instead of leading them into battle . . . tell them to go back to hibernation. Can you do that?"

"Wait! *Can* he do that?" Oliver asks.

Regina ignores him and continues, "If you send them back to hibernation underground, that'll be a good way to start fresh between us. Okay? Tell them zombie season's over for the year. It's done."

Regina sees Oliver's expression go from confusion to something halfway between awe and horror. "Is this for real?"

Regina stays focused on Nix, who seems to understand what she's asking.

"What do you say, Nix?" she asks. "It'll go a long way to making up for everything you did last time."

This is a big moment, she realizes. Will the zombie cooperate with what she wants? If he refuses to help, he's not going to make the right sort of impact as a witness-slash-victim of Sky Stone's crimes against humanity.

But Nix nods, and he clenches his awful fingers into fists. He closes his eyes and strains.

Regina tenses as the silence stretches on.

As she waits, Regina looks at Nix more closely, and sees how small he looks now, compared to how he is in her memory. How fragile, somehow.

A breathy sound emerges from Nix's throat, and Regina stiffens.

He shakes his head. "Too far," he says weakly.

Oliver gasps at the sound. "He *can* talk," says Oliver.

Nix looks at Oliver like he's insulted. He doesn't say anything else, though.

"They're too far away?" Regina asks. "Is that it, Nix?"

Nix nods.

Oliver's eyebrows lift. "But if we get you closer?" he asks. "Then you could—"

"Regina," says Nix.

Regina feels the hairs on the back of her neck stand up. "Yes, Nix?"

"Can I stay?" Nix asks.

Stay. That was the first thing he said to her when they met. And yet, the way he said it then couldn't have been more different from the way he says it now.

With that one question, she can feel how much has changed for Nix in the past few weeks. For one thing, he's not *telling*, he's *asking*. It's not a command, it's a request. It means *help me*. It means *I'm sorry*. It means *I understand*.

Regina marvels. These are things that even an intelligent zombie should not be able to say. To say it *all*, with one word? There's no way to deny there's humanity in it.

It makes Regina's puzzle mind start to work overtime: Whatever's happening to Nix, he's more human than before.

"When's the last time he ate anything?" Regina asks Oliver curiously.

"We haven't fed him since yesterday. And even then, we had to convince him."

Regina considers this. That bottomless hunger that all zombies share . . . it's hardly there at all. She needs to get to Stuxville and see for herself. What if Nix is even more valuable than as a way to take out Sky Stone? What if he's the key to everything?

"Okay," says Regina. "Listen. Oliver—"

Regina hears something from outside her bedroom door, and knows she needs to get off the call.

"I'll do my best to help Redwood, okay? You and I can talk more when I get there. I'm coming as fast as I can."

Oliver nods. "I'll be here," he says.

"Okay," says Regina. "Just—I need you, Ollie. Please don't give up on this before I get there?"

"I'm not going anywhere," he promises.

21

THE DEAD ZONE

In the mess hall on the *Undercurrent*, Kai Stone has introduced a card game that's immediately captured the fascination of the group. As soon as one game ends, another begins. There's always a circle of kids playing, it seems.

Anton was naturally interested, of course, his competitive nature outweighing his dislike for the ringleader. But after struggling and struggling to understand the rules, Anton has officially given up.

The rules of this game, Kai insists, do actually exist, but as far as Anton can tell, there is no logic to them—they're random and silly and actually really mean . . . because anyone who *doesn't* follow the rules is penalized for their ignorance.

"Seriously?" Anton bursts out after being given a series of penalty cards for some inexplicable reason.

"Penalty, talking," says Kai, with an oily shrug of non-apology.

"It's like the whole point of the game is to punish people!" Anton says, flinging his cards away. "Why do you guys even *like* this?"

Anton scans the faces of Kai's followers, who all watch Anton in silence.

It feels like they're all mocking him. Judging him.

Until his eyes reach Joule's. She, too, is silent, but there's no amusement in her expression. Half the reason Anton stuck out the game this long is because she's playing, too. He doesn't understand why she's spending so much time hanging around with Kai.

But as Anton locks eyes with her, she stands up to leave.

"Know what?" says Joule. "I'm out, too."

"Joule, come on!" says Kai. "It's just how the game—"

"Penalty, talking," Joule cuts him off, handing Kai her whole pile of cards.

As the group reacts with silent glee, Kai glares at her and accepts his penalty. Forced to abide by his own rules.

Anton is so keenly focused on Kai's unexpected embarrassment that he doesn't even notice Joule turn and walk away. He only notices when she's halfway to the door of the mess hall.

"Joule? Hey, wait," Anton calls. He rushes to catch up. "Thanks."

"I don't know why you hang out with that kid so much," says Joule.

Anton frowns. "Me? You're always around him when I see you."

Joule presses her lips together. "I promised I would," she answers with an annoyed tone. "I told my friend Regina I'd keep an eye on him. She thinks he's up to something. Probably something with Vic Pinkerton and those crates, I'm guessing."

Anton feels his face get warm. As they walk, he attempts to hide the fact that it's not Kai who is doing sneaky things with Vic—it's actually Anton himself.

"Let's go see how the dive is going," Joule suggests. "A game with rules that are actually *fun* to learn."

"Great idea," says Anton.

But in the control center, the mood is much different from how it was when they first arrived and Dr. Aldi got upset with an octopus for tangling with the camera.

Things have gotten much more serious all of a sudden.

"There!" Professor Halyard peers closely at a small monitor displaying video from the remote-controlled submarine. It seems to have everyone in the control center captivated, but up in the gallery where Anton stands, it's just a gloomy darkness.

There's no day or night this far down, Anton knows. No change of temperature from one season to the next. It's all the same, all the time.

There's nothing to see at all, really. Just a deserted expanse.

And that's the most upsetting part.

Anton gets chills from looking at it.

For a reason he can't name, it's like looking at a haunted house. Only not the kind you want to go in on Halloween. A real one.

"There, you see?" says Halyard, pointing to the monitor. But there's still nothing there that Anton can discern.

Everywhere the camera moves, there's just more nothing. No fish or crabs and kelp. Nothing but a thick greenish fog, illuminated by a faint light.

"Wait. I see it, too," says Dr. Aldi as he steers the *Fluke*.

Gradually, Anton realizes that this isn't light from the submarine's headlamp. The light is coming from something on the ocean floor.

And the researchers below are trying to peer at something *inside* the fog.

"This is bad," says Dr. Aldi.

"This is perfect," Professor Halyard replies. "It's why we're out here. To explore. Dig deeper into the truth of our strange and wonderful world.

"We need to get closer," Halyard insists.

"Trying, Hugo. I'm at the ROV's top speed."

"Then why's it taking this long, Aldo?"

"Because it's far away," Dr. Aldi says.

Slowly, it changes, as the submarine gets closer.

It takes a very long time to see inside the fog, but eventually there's an eerie movement in the yellow-green light on the seafloor.

And Anton feels his guts twist into a knot.

He's seen this before.

He remembers the fishing boat. The irresistibly powerful deep-sea zombie. His cousin Alek's expression in those terrified final moments.

The fog is teeming with deep-sea-dwelling zombies just like that, Anton realizes.

With eerie, steady slowness, it moves over itself. Like an enormous oily amoeba that gathers in all the food it can reach. Swallowing anything it can envelop.

"Light, in the most hopeless of places," Professor Halyard muses, watching the video feed. The strange light casts his face in a ghastly pallor. It's a strange expression, given the situation. It's like he just won the lottery.

"Well, folks, it's definitely a dead zone," Halyard finally declares. "A horde of amphibious undead. Their supercooled blood makes that fog when they draw the heat into themselves—"

The submarine gets closer.

"I can't believe we found it on our first dive," says Dr. Aldi.

Professor Halyard shrugs. "Humanity may have a renewed sense of safety on land, but it seems the seafloor may quickly be turning into a wasteland."

Anton feels a shiver of fear down his back.

"Slow and steady," says Professor Halyard.

Anton isn't sure if he's talking about Dr. Aldi's piloting, or the zombies' progress in devouring all life on Earth.

He turns to look at Joule—and he sees that she's got tears in her eyes.

He freezes in place, totally without an idea what to do in this situation. After a long moment of uncertainty, he clears his throat to get her attention.

"Hey, are you okay?" he asks her.

She nods yes, but it's not very convincing.

He remembers what she told him about the beach in New York.

"When you saw it come on land," he asks, "did you lose someone?"

For a moment, she tries to answer. But it's too hard, Anton can see.

"I get it," says Anton. "On the fishing boat, I did, too . . . my cousin Alek. I saw it happen."

Anton sees Joule's eyes open wide at this confession. It makes things even worse, he sees. *Wrong call, Zarkovsky*, he thinks, looking at the ground.

He thinks about what would help him feel better in this situation. He keeps coming back to the sight of Vic Pinkerton and Sky Stone bringing down that giant zombie in Munivit. How much better he felt, knowing that smart people were inventing new zombiefighting tools. That one of those tools is right here on the ship with them.

Can I trust her? Anton thinks to himself.

But just then there's a voice calling his name. "Anton!"

He looks up and sees Pinkerton standing behind him, looming in annoyance.

"Follow me," she commands, moving fast.

———

"Okay, Zarkovsky," she says, leading Anton to the deck of the ship. "You know what I'm *really* here for, right? I'm not providing security, like we told everyone. Not exactly."

"I think everybody's figured that out," says Anton, watching with great interest as Pinkerton climbs aboard the other submarine on the *Undercurrent*. The deep-sea exploration vehicle—which everyone calls the DSV—that can take humans down to the seafloor.

"Are you sure you're allowed in there?" Anton asks.

"This expedition is funded by HumaniTeam, and Sky sent me here on a mission for the company—so that gives me the authority to do anything I want here. And my standing orders to you are to do anything I tell you to, without asking questions."

"Yes, ma'am."

"Good," says Pinkerton. "The truth is: I'm here to test another invention that Sky rescued from the archives. Same principle as the one you saw in Alaska, but it's more like a depth charge. Designed for multiple targets. We think if we can get it in the middle of that dead zone, we can knock them all out at once."

As Pinkerton explains, she unpacks one of the crates that she brought aboard to reveal a machine that looks very different from what was used to incapacitate the zombie in Munivit.

This version looks more like a bomb.

It fits neatly onto a specimen-collection arm, which acts like a grappling claw on the front of the submarine.

"Nobody can know it's happening until it's already done," says Pinkerton with a serious frown. "Got it?"

He blinks. "Not even Professor Halyard?"

"Especially not him. Nothing can get in the way of our progress."

"Wait," says Anton. "No one on the ship knows what you're about to do?"

"They'll see it on their monitors. Won't that be a nice surprise? Don't ruin it for them."

Unbidden, Anton's imagination produces a snapshot of Joule getting to experience for herself how it felt when Anton saw the Eel in action in Munivit.

He smiles, and Pinkerton smiles back.

"Here's your job," she says. "Listen up. The DSV needs two people to launch. Me inside, piloting. And someone out here, pressing these three buttons."

Very clearly, she shows him three large buttons: red, amber, and blue.

"You press the first to unlock the cradle, then you press the second to automatically swing the cradle over the water. The third button lowers the vessel into the water. Got it?"

"No problem."

"Okay. Touch *nothing* else—tell *no one* else."

With that, she climbs into the submarine and closes the hatch.

Anton presses the red button, and there's a loud *clank*.

The second button tips the whole submarine off the edge of the ship.

The third button unspools a thick cable, lowering the vessel into the sea, where it quickly dives, sinking like a rock, out of sight.

Anton stands on the deck, tensed for anything. As if every fiber of his being is charged with electricity.

22

PROJECT REGINA

"Dad. I need to talk to you."

Regina's father looks up from cleaning the kitchen.

She glances around and triple-checks they're alone now.

She already knows they are, of course: Sky slipped away approximately two minutes after getting what he wanted from the Herreras. And Regina's mother is rushing out of the house, on the phone with Chief Wachs. Telling Oliver's aunt why there won't be a Cloudbuster launch to save Redwood tonight, and that she's got an "audacious alternative to discuss."

"What does that mean?" Regina asks.

"Relax," her father says. "Mom knows what she's doing."

"Does she?" says Regina. "Going back to work for Sky and HumaniTeam? After everything they did to her? Everything he did to the world?"

Regina is mad about this for many reasons. But not least of them is that it means that her parents won't have any interest whatsoever in exposing HumaniTeam's crimes. Not after Dr. Herrera's deal with the devil. It's infuriating.

"Hey. Hey," says Mr. Herrera. "We wouldn't have survived the Dusk this long if people like Sky and your mom didn't know how to somehow manage their differences."

"But what Sky is doing is making it *impossible* to survive zombie season. He's evil."

Her father neatly folds the dishrag he's using to wipe the counters, and looks Regina in the eye. "Regina, can we take a second to appreciate the fact that your mother just managed to take control of Project Cloudbuster?"

"And what good is that, if Sky's her boss?"

"It means when she warns the world about the dangers of the technology, they'll actually listen, for one thing," says Mr. Herrera. "But even more important? It means she controls the launches. No one understands the enormous consequences like she does. She can make sure they're only used in a true emergency."

For a moment, Regina feels relieved as she realizes that her dad is right. But then she remembers Project Coloma. Herreras make mistakes just like anyone else. All humans do.

Regina's father can see her struggling with this.

"Do you have a better solution, Regina? We can't just let the zombies devour the world."

Regina hesitates. *I do have a better solution*, she wants to say, imagining Nix telling the horde to disengage. To go back into hibernation.

"You need to trust us, Regina," lectures Mr. Herrera. "Solutions are messy things when people are all so different. It takes time, and faith—"

"All I see is that Sky is an even *bigger* problem now, Dad. He's CEO. And that means there's no one to stop him from creating new disasters—ten Project Cloudbusters, a hundred different Project Phoenixes. He has to be stopped."

"What exactly do you know about Project Phoenix?" says Mr. Herrera sharply.

Regina gathers her courage, weighing her words.

"I'm on your team, Gina," he tells her, more gently. "You know that, right? The part of my work that matters most to me is Project Regina."

She nods, remembering how he's taking time away from his job—keeping up Regina's education through homeschooling. Setting aside important matters of his own, helping her and giving her support every day. Without her father, Regina wouldn't be where she is right now.

Regina's mouth is suddenly dry, her stomach twisting in a knot. It's too late to stop now.

"Okay, I have a confession to make, Dad. Ever since Project Coloma went wrong, I've been trying to figure out how it happened. How the NRG could've failed. And what I learned . . . is that the problem happened a long time *before* Project Coloma. It started with Project Phoenix . . ."

"Your mother told me about your suspicions," her father says with deliberate calm.

"They're not *suspicions*, Dad. There's proof."

Her father sinks into himself. "I don't need to see proof," he says.

"You don't think it's important to punish the people who did an experiment like that? Who somehow created a zombie who can strategize and command the others like an army, and then dumped him in a prison, where he started one of the worst zombie waves in history?"

Regina's father's face registers surprise. "Did you say *command*?"

"Yes," says Regina.

Regina's father thinks, clearly surprised by this revelation.

"And if he can command a zombie army to attack," Regina continues, "he can command a zombie horde to retreat. Right?"

"I have no idea how to answer that question," Mr. Herrera says. "But, Regina . . . what exactly makes you think that a zombie from Project Phoenix was responsible for the destruction of the NRG?"

Regina hesitates.

She can almost hear Joule in her head, saying, *Trust people if you want them to trust you.*

"Okay, Dad. What if I told you I *met* the zombie commander who led the Rogue Wave in Redwood?"

Regina's father takes a hard look at Regina.

Regina presses on. "What if I told you we can *talk* to him? What if I told you I know where he is right now?" Before her father can come up with a reply to this, she continues: "Dad, he's the answer. He can take command of the horde that's out there *right now*. Tell them to go back to hibernation. To return to their hiding places, underground."

For a moment, her father seems a little disturbed. Rethinking something.

"Dad?" says Regina. "Are you hearing me? I'm saying we can end zombie season without a single Cloudbuster."

"Hold on, Gina," says Mr. Herrera. "Let's back up and take one thing at a time. Okay? First of all, HumaniTeam didn't *create* them."

Rapidly, a sequence of dominoes topples in Regina's puzzle brain. "You were *part* of it. That's why you—you—"

He waits, continuing to listen to her silence as much as he listened to her words.

"How could you be a part of that, Dad?" Regina asks, her voice rising to a shout.

"Let me explain. What you know as Project Phoenix started at another company that HumaniTeam took over."

"Another company?" says Regina. Regina knows, vaguely, that HumaniTeam and a smaller rival combined forces years ago. Two companies became one. She doesn't really know much more than that. Except for one thing:

The rival company was run by Sky Stone.

Regina's father locks eyes with her, seeing her mind catching up. "When the deal was done, *that's* when we were told about Project Phoenix. Buried in a huge document, the size of an encyclopedia. And so: Then it was our responsibility. Our people, me included . . . we fought and fought against Sky and his supporters to get it shut down. We succeeded, eventually. And until your discovery, I thought there was nothing left of the project."

Regina thinks about this, uncertain what to believe.

"And now that it's out there, I really need you to understand something," her father says firmly. "Experimenting on people like that is wrong. Period."

"Experimenting on *people*?" says Regina. "You believe zombies are people."

Regina's father looks uncomfortable. "I do, Regina. But proving it with experiments like Phoenix goes against my moral code. Because if there's something left of the person inside that supernatural monster—if you actually connect to some kernel of humanity—that means zombies are actually just like us, deep down. Somewhere. Imagine if it were you, in that horrible prison . . ."

"I know it's wrong," says Regina, unable to listen to any more. It's too easy for Regina to imagine being trapped in that nightmarish existence herself. Whatever kernel of zombification Nix noticed about her earlier that summer, what if it's still inside her somewhere?

"And on top of that, being experimented on . . ."

"I can imagine it, Dad," says Regina. "I get it."

"Good," he says. "Even if you're genuinely trying to do a good thing. It's wrong and it'll destroy you in the process."

"So, someone like that . . . you don't think we can help them, Dad?"

"That's a different question," says her father carefully. "If you see something good inside another human—I prefer to believe there is always a way to help."

Regina lets out a silent breath, feeling a tiny bit of relief. Her father might've known about Project Phoenix, but he was on the right side.

"So," her father says. "You were saying that one of the zombies who was part of the project still exists? And that you found him?"

"His name is Nix," says Regina. "I've got him hidden away right now. But we need to go get him *tonight*, if we're going to stop the horde without using Cloudbusters."

"Exactly where did you hide him, Regina?"

23

THE DEAD ZONE, PART 2

As Joule stands in the gallery, watching the video being sent back from the *Fluke's* camera, Anton returns and takes a spot beside her.

"Hey," he says. "You okay?"

"Yeah." She pauses. "I'm so sorry about Alek."

He nods, holding her look. "Thanks, Joule."

She clears her throat. "It was my dad. The person who I lost. I've been wondering what he'd think if he saw this." She points at the screen, showing the dead zone on the seafloor.

It stretches away into the endless darkness on every side of the *Fluke*. A writhing mass of human-seeming eyes and elbows, torsos and teeth, it almost seems to be a single organism, glowing an eerie yellow-green.

She shrugs it off wearily. "So, what'd Pinkerton want?"

"You'll see for yourself very soon," Anton replies with an encouraging smile. "And if it's anything like what I saw her do back in Munivit, it'll make you feel much better about what's on that video screen."

He points at the images from the uncrewed research sub thousands of feet underneath where the *Undercurrent* now floats.

Joule sees that he's trying to help, but she can't let Anton's enthusiasm go unanswered. "You know that your pals at HumaniTeam are the cause of the dead zone down there, right?"

Instantly, Anton's smile disappears. "Is that what your friend Regina Herrera told you?"

Now Joule stiffens. She doesn't answer.

"Know what?" says Anton. "For someone who's alive now because Cloudbusters stopped the zombie wave at her doorstep, you're awful eager to label Sky Stone a bad guy."

Joule feels the truth in this, but then she remembers what Regina unearthed about the horrific Project Phoenix. "You have no idea some of the things Sky Stone has done."

"You'd be surprised what I know," says Anton proudly, turning away.

He stares at the video from far beneath the surface.

With an aching regret, Joule mentally crosses Anton off the list for Team Regina, and stares out as well.

Joule suddenly gets this image in her mind of an enormous eye looking up. As if the dead zone seems to watch *it* as keenly as the ROV is watching *them*.

It's unsettling, but she fights the urge to turn away. She resists the urge to give in to hopelessness that's rising again now, like the tide that lifted the whale into the surf that day at the beach . . .

This must have been what the whale saw when she was hunting for food. A green-yellow light, luring her in. Thinking it was a meal, diving with her huge mouth like an aircraft hangar, open wide. Along the ocean floor teeming with zombies, swimming and skimming, inhaling seawater and anything that was in it.

A final poisonous meal, though she didn't know that yet.

Joule feels a jolt of adrenaline go through her. It supercharges the memory as she once more sees the surfers all gathered together, calling out "Help!" and disappearing under the waves, one by one.

Looking at the dead zone far below, Joule imagines each and every one of those zombies rampaging. She imagines the gentle things they will destroy. The kind people who will try to help, and be the first to lose their lives as a result.

What a fool she is to come out here looking for hope, Joule thinks.

She turns to the door and rushes out of the gallery, feeling way too closed in, inside this ship.

"Joule?" Anton calls after her.

"I gotta get some air," she tells him.

"Want some company?" he asks.

"Maybe later," she says.

"Okay, I'll be here." Anton retreats, stung.

On the deck of the ship, Joule takes a deep breath of clean nighttime air. She still feels dizzy. Still trapped in the memory of the awful, awful day at Rockaway Beach.

It's the early hours of the morning, she's startled to discover.

And to her surprise, she's not alone. Kai is already up here, standing by the rail.

"Kai?" she says.

"Hey," says Kai. "Wait'll you hear this one, Joule. Vic Pinkerton was just up here with your pal Anton Zarkovsky. Doing *something* with a submarine and the crates Vic brought . . . Want to help me spy on them?"

"I'm just going to stand here quietly, if that's okay," says Joule.

"That's mostly what spying is," says Kai with a grin.

Joule sags against the railing. She presses the heels of her hands into her eyes and rubs. Squeezing her brain from the outside as she feels her frustration squeezing from within.

She wants Kai to leave, but she's too tired to argue. Too tired to do anything. The texts she got from Regina earlier this evening are still fresh in her memory, though. Describing the full extent of Kai's betrayal. That Sky told Regina that *Kai* reported back on everything Regina was doing in Redwood. This is all on top of Kai failing the basic test of human decency by rebuilding the NRG.

And on one hand, she has no interest in talking about it with Kai. But on the other hand? "You wanna hear something funny, Kai?" says Joule.

"Sure," says Kai.

"So, your dad just told Regina how you spied on her in Redwood."

"He *told* her?" says Kai unhappily.

Joule looks at him hard. "Which part are you upset about? That you did a really crappy thing or that she found out about it?"

"How's this supposed to be funny?" Kai asks, dodging the question.

"That's not what's funny. What's funny is that when she told *me* about what you did, she asked me to push you overboard at my earliest convenience . . . and here we are."

She gestures to where they stand, at the rail of the ship.

"It's so tempting. It'd be so easy."

"You wouldn't," says Kai.

"It's almost like fate," she suggests.

In the bright moonlight, Joule's eyes spot a flutter of movement in the water, next to where the submarine's tough umbilical cable enters the water, stretching from the ship all the way down to the *Fluke* in the depths of the sea. A wisp of fog drifting up off the water, clinging to the cable as it's borne like a kite into the sky by the sea breeze that never ends. Joule dismisses it.

Joule smiles. "Come on, do I look like I'd do that?"

Kai eyes her warily. "In my experience, people who do sneaky things are usually clever enough to know they shouldn't *look* like they do sneaky things."

"They're also probably clever enough to not *tell* you if they're actually thinking about attempting to push you into a zombie dead zone, Kai."

Kai nods, accepting this logic.

"Your dad said one more thing, too, actually," Joule adds.

Kai sags. "I was *really* hoping I could get away from my dad out here."

"I'm ready to go back to standing here quietly anytime, Kai."

"What else did the great, magnificent, all-knowing Sky Stone say?" Kai says with a deep frustration.

"He said that the whole coastline is in danger of being attacked by zombies like the ones under us. That the dead zone down there is just one of many. The zombies are *everywhere*."

Kai, too pale to turn any more pale, starts to look seasick. "That part I knew, actually."

"You *knew*?"

"That's why he wanted me to come on this expedition. So I'd be safe, when the surge arrived."

"While countless other people are just hearing tonight what's coming for them," says Joule in disgust. "I'm so tired of people fighting *against* each other and not *for* each other, Kai."

Joule feels a violent shudder go through her whole body as a cold breeze blows into her. There's a cloud of white that comes out of her mouth, like a ghost just passed through her—

But as soon as she notices it, it's gone.

Kai shudders, too, Joule sees.

"I *thought* the reason I came out here was to learn how to fight the bad guys. To figure out how to do that out *here* before they come attack *us*," Joule adds, half to herself and half to Kai. "But the problem with my plan is that we can't win a fight against the zombies, no matter where it's fought. They'll just keep coming. What we're fighting, Kai—it's *us*."

With that, Joule turns away.

Leaving Kai behind, she heads inside, alone. She doesn't even look back.

Lost in her own thoughts as she passes through the door that leads belowdecks and to the girls' bunk, Joule doesn't notice the wisp of fog in the moonlight that slips in just behind her, before the door clangs shut and locks.

Later, Joule will realize that that was the last time anyone on the boat saw Kai Stone before he went missing.

It will take a depressingly long time for anyone to get worried about him, unfortunately.

24

WRAITHS

Anton wishes Joule were here.

He wants a do-over at some of the harsh words he said, for one thing.

And he doesn't want her to miss out on witnessing Vic Pinkerton's successful test of HumaniTeam's newest zombiefighting triumph, either.

Anton is sure that Joule's wrong about the company. But after getting to know her, he's certain that her heart is in the right place.

He wonders what Alek would say about Anton's promise to Sky to keep quiet about what he saw. To help Vic with her secret mission. It's a lot of sneaking around, hiding important things from people who deserve to know what's *really* going on around them.

On the monitor, video of the dead zone that's thousands of feet directly below them is captured in great detail. A mass of tangled-up zombies, all on top of each other. He can see the faces and fingers, teeth and toes. Climbing on top of one another, reaching out toward the *Fluke* as it gets closer and closer . . . almost within reach.

But these zombies aren't like the powerful giants he saw. These zombies are skinny. Starved. Blown about by the current of the water.

Below, Dr. Aldi and Professor Halyard examine them in fascination and horror, and Anton listens to their conversation . . .

"They're like some sort of wraiths," Dr. Aldi remarks.

"Did you say *wraiths*?" asks Halyard.

Dr. Aldi peers closely at his screen. "They're thin. Like they're starving. Beyond starving. Fading into the fog itself."

"Is there hibernation season in the ocean?" asks Halyard.

"Good question," says Dr. Aldi. "But since the water down here is the same temperature all year round no matter the season, there might not be."

"So, what happens when there's nothing to feed on, and there's no way to conserve energy by hibernating?"

"I wish we could raise one of them up to the ship to see a little closer," says Dr. Aldi.

"Don't even *joke* about that, Aldo."

As if hypnotized, Dr. Aldi coaxes the *Fluke* closer and closer to the seafloor, where the dead zone is.

In response, they move closer and closer to the *Fluke*. Stretching out their sticky, slimy fingers.

But then something else speeds through the background of the frame, and Professor Halyard suddenly tenses. "Hold on. What was that? Go right. Is that . . . ?"

Dr. Aldi uses the camera controls to pan and follow the speeding object and center it in the frame: a familiar submersible. The one Pinkerton commandeered.

Professor Halyard gasps, filling with a chilling rage. "What is the *Snail* doing down there?" he demands. "Did you authorize this, Aldo?"

Dr. Aldi looks shocked, too. "I have no idea what's happening, Hugo."

Halyard turns to face the entire room, his fury making everyone freeze. "Does anyone know why my crewed submarine is diving into the middle of an extremely dangerous dead zone?!"

Anton feels an intense cold run through his veins, but he doesn't speak.

"Nobody?!" Halyard shouts. "Aldo, get the pilot on the radio, right now."

"Relax, Hugo. I'm right here," Vic Pinkerton's voice pipes in over the speakers.

"Pinkerton?" says Halyard. "Explain this act of piracy. Right now."

"I'm on a mission authorized by the CEO of the company that funds this entire expedition, so cool off, please."

As Halyard and Pinkerton face off, Anton is distracted by a flutter of motion across the camera lens. "What was that?" he asks.

Nobody answers.

"Hey. Did you see that, Joule?" Anton asks.

But when Anton glances in Joule's direction, he remembers that she's no longer there.

Frustrated, he keeps his eyes peeled, watching the monitor. Maybe he's imagining things?

But then there's another flitter of movement. This time Anton's ready. "Professor Halyard!" he calls out.

Halyard waves for Anton to be quiet.

Anton can't be quiet. It's a zombie. Leaping up onto the *Fluke*.

It climbs past the camera. Out of view.

"Dr. Aldi!" says Anton. "Play back the video!"

"Eh?" Dr. Aldi says, distracted.

"There's a zombie on the *Fluke*," says Anton.

"What now?" Dr. Aldi demands crankily. "Anton . . ."

"There's a zombie on the ROV, Dr. Aldi," Anton says, as calmly and evenly as he's able. "It just went past the camera."

Instantly, Dr. Aldi works the controls to lift the *Fluke* farther away from the seafloor. Away from the zombies, stretching out their arms . . .

As Dr. Aldi plays back the video, he sees what Anton did.

Pinkerton interrupts. "I can see it from here, folks. It's moving up the tether."

"Can those things climb the tether?" asks Professor Halyard.

"That's exactly what I'm watching it do," says Pinkerton.

"We're under attack?" asks Professor Halyard.

"Relax, folks," says Pinkerton. "I can take care of this. Keep those cameras rolling, and watch this—"

Suddenly, Pinkerton's audio cuts out and static comes from the speakers

A moment later, all the instruments on the *Fluke* go offline at once.

As Anton watches, the video from the *Fluke* flashes white and then turns to static, too.

Throughout the *Undercurrent*, there is stunned silence.

25

VANILLA AND GHOST PEPPER

DUSK ALERT: A dead zone moving down the Canadian coast into the waters of the Pacific Northwest will begin to surge in the coming hours. All coastal areas must immediately evacuate. Seek the highest ground available, 100 feet above sea level, at least two miles from the nearest shoreline, riverfront, or bay. Open water will be extremely treacherous.

As Oliver finishes reading the notification on his phone, a shiver travels from his brain to the base of his spine. But he stays focused on his mission.

One foot in front of the other, Oliver reminds himself.

The best thing Oliver can do to make a difference is protect Nix. After what he witnessed on the video call that evening, he is beginning to believe that Regina's right—that Nix could be the key to figuring out a way to solve the zombie problem for good. Nix is not like the others, it's perfectly clear.

For the first time in ages, Oliver feels like he's in the right place, right now. He feels like he's luckier than he deserves to be, getting this opportunity to do something important. It's the kind of heroics he was given credit for when he came to Stuxville—but this time around, he feels less like an impostor. He's growing into the idea that he can make a difference—because of the team he and Regina have become.

And that team needs to grow. Not only do they have to continue to protect Nix from the HumaniTeam security forces hunting for him, they have to get him to Redwood to stop the horde—and then get him *out* of Redwood, undetected . . .

They need Del, Oliver realizes. Someone they can trust—and someone keen to do something that matters, even if it's risky. So Oliver picks up the pace as he crosses the campus, looking for Del, who isn't answering his texts. Heading inside the dorm, he finds everyone *but* his best friend all jammed together in the lobby, anxiously discussing the two approaching zombie hordes.

Oliver hurries toward the elevator, on his way up to the room where Del's family is staying. But halfway across the room, Oliver's attention catches on Del's friend Milo's voice:

"Like, make up your mind, right? Which flavor of zombies do you want us to evacuate from *more*? The original vanilla kind on land? Or the new ones in the water? My uncle up near Seattle sent me a video of what's happening up there. That's not a good vibe, either. That's like *ghost pepper* flavor. Or Carolina Reaper."

"Vanilla and ghost pepper, two great flavors together at last," says Oliver, with as friendly a smile as he can manage. "I'm just looking for Del. Have you seen him?"

"He was in the group text five minutes ago," says Conrad. "Is he not answering your texts or something?"

Oliver's expression darkens.

Conrad laughs. "Hey, listen, sorry about Redwood. Really sucks to know you're never, ever going home again. Did you see the pictures?"

Before Oliver knows what's happening, Conrad shoves a phone in his face and shows Oliver helicopter video footage of what is unmistakably Redwood, already beyond saving. Reduced to cinder blocks and dust. Even the river is dry.

Oliver feels something inside him break. *It's too late.*

"*Relax*, Conrad," Milo says sharply. Oliver barely hears it.

The numbness in Oliver spreads from his fingers to his chest, and there's a ringing sound in his ears. There's a taste in the back of his mouth. Something bitter. But it's not the images that caused this reaction. It's what happened just before that . . .

"Hey, Conrad?" Oliver says, barely a croak. "What did I do to hurt Del?"

"You really wanna know?" Conrad asks.

"Stop, Conrad," says Milo. "He's with his dad, at the medical center. Room three twenty."

"The medical center?" says Oliver, with a rising confusion and worry.

"Zombie bites are tough to heal from," says Milo.

Oliver's stomach drops.

"Zombie bites?"

He remembers how Del's father was injured in Redwood during the Rogue Wave. But Del never mentioned that it was so severe. Oliver just assumed he'd gotten better. And yet, it suddenly makes a little more sense why Del has been so eager to become a better zombiefighter.

After Milo admits he doesn't know anything else, Oliver flat-out sprints to the Stuxville Medical Center two blocks away. After dashing up the stairs, he searches the hospital hallway for room 320.

Catching his breath, Oliver gently knocks. "Hello?"

"C'mon in," says a man's voice.

Oliver peers inside and spots Mr. Shorter in the hospital bed, awake, watching the news about the dead zone, which an on-screen graphic is calling "the supersurge." He looks a lot skinnier than the last time Oliver saw him.

In the chair next to the bed, his head tipped deeply to the side, is Del. Asleep, in the least comfortable position imaginable, with a cadet aptitude exam book on his lap.

Del's father waves Oliver inside. "Hey, Ollie. Good to see ya."

Del doesn't stir as Oliver comes inside. "Hi, Mr. Shorter. How are you feeling?"

"I'm good, Ollie. Thanks."

"You've been in the hospital all this time?" Oliver asks. "Since we evacuated from Redwood?"

Del's father looks surprised. "Zombie wounds get infected sometimes, it's just the way it goes. Coulda been way worse if you and your dad hadn't found us when you did, pal," says Mr. Shorter. Then, with a note of concern, he asks, "Del didn't tell you what was going on?"

He's talking as much to his son as to Oliver, noticing this crack in the friendship between the boys with concern.

"No, he didn't," Oliver answers, eyeing Mr. Shorter for signs of zombi-fication. He must be pretty obvious about it, because Mr. Shorter laughs.

"Ollie, relax. I'm not gonna turn into a zombie because I got a scratch. That's not how it works."

In the chair beside the bed, Del yawns, then adjusts his position. "You don't know that, Dad. Everyone has their theories where zombies come from."

"If it were as logical as 'infected people turn into zombies,' scientists would've figured *that* out a long time ago," Mr. Shorter says.

"That's true," Oliver agrees. "Hey, Del."

"Hey, Ollie. What's going on? Are we evacuating?"

"Can't, nowhere to go," Oliver says, repeating to Del what Milo said before, about the vanilla flavor coming this way through the hills, and the ghost pepper flavor creating treacherous waters up and down the entire coastline.

Del's dad laughs, and praises Oliver's impression of Milo as spot-on, but Del doesn't really notice. He just thinks about it for a minute, sets his jaw, and nods. "Well, I guess we're making our stand here in Stuxville, then, huh?" Oliver barely has time to process Del's super casual declaration of war against two zombie hordes before Del pushes his study materials off his lap and springs to his feet.

"Let's go, then, Ollie. See ya, Dad!"

Oliver says a hurried goodbye to Mr. Shorter and follows. Del isn't waiting for him, it's clear.

Oliver can barely catch up with Del's double-time speed walk. "Hey, can we talk, Del? Why didn't you tell me your dad was sick?"

"Why didn't you ask?" Del replies.

Oliver distinctly remembers texting Del in the days between their evacuation from Redwood and their arrival in Stuxville. Del was always really evasive. Just like he's being right now. "I'm pretty sure I tried to talk to you a lot of times, Del."

"Ollie. We don't have time for this. The guys are waiting."

Oliver stops moving quite so fast. Letting Del get ahead of him.

"Come on, Ollie!" Del urges. "This is what we've been training for. There are plans in place, you know. Stashes of supplies. Bait. Water. We even managed to get a C-pack."

Oliver slows down even more.

"It's kinda for the best that we can't run away this time, I think," Del chatters on. "My dad and the rest of the people in the hospital wouldn't be able to evacuate either way. At least this way we're all fighting together."

Oliver stops in his tracks. Drawing a line.

"Del. I really want to talk. But if you just want to *run away*, that's your choice."

Del stops. He turns to face Oliver, finally meeting his best friend's eye.

"Ollie, look . . ." says Del.

Oliver can feel Del at war with himself. Struggling to be who he thinks he ought to be—not who he really is.

But then Del's gaze shifts, seeing something behind Oliver.

"Ollie? *Look*," says Del, pointing at a long line of zombiefighting vehicles, accelerating up the street toward the campus.

They're not brigadiers like his aunt, Oliver sees as the first truck comes to a stop right where he and Del are standing. They're all private security, from HumaniTeam.

"Cavalry's here, kids," calls out the closest of the zombiefighters. "Come on back to the zomb shelter with me. We'll take it from here."

And though the zombiefighter seems to suggest that they're here to protect the community, Oliver feels a prickle of fear.

Oliver's eyes instantly go to the library, where Nix is hiding.

Three of the other trucks light it up with huge spotlights, and there are probably twenty people in C-packs spilling out on all sides around it. Turning the whole area upside down, searching for something . . .

HumaniTeam is closing in on Nix. They seem to know *exactly* where he is.

Without another word, Oliver sprints toward the library.

The zombiefighter calls out, "Hey, kid!" and tries to chase him down.

But unlike Del, Oliver is very good at Manhunt.

26

CARROT AND STICK

As Regina and her father speed along the highway, adrenaline pulses in her veins. She finally feels like things are all coming together for her. Even if it's not exactly how Regina planned. By convincing Nix to call off the invading zombie hordes, she's doing something even bigger than punishing Sky. She's working toward a real solution.

She imagines all the lives they'll save, the destruction they'll prevent . . . and that's just the *beginning.*

The theory that Nix might be able to escape the nightmare of his monstrous existence keeps running through her brain. But first, she needs to get to Stuxville and collect Nix, and take him to Redwood so he can end the zombie rampage. It's all happening so fast now . . . it's hard to believe it's real.

Regina's breakthrough with Nix could completely change the way the world sees zombies. He may be the key to solving the whole zombie problem.

She tries not to get ahead of herself, though. First she has to deal with the two hordes closing in on San Francisco Bay—one from the land, and one from the sea.

The telltale spike of heat and smell of zombie bodies reminds her of the situation's enormous danger.

"Are we there yet?" she asks impatiently.

"Almost," says her father.

But when the car turns off the highway, Regina's excitement turns to total confusion.

It's very clear they're not in Stuxville. They're at some sort of airfield, surrounded by zombieproofing and barbed wire fences. There's a sign marking the site as a decommissioned naval air station, and a brighter sign with both the California zombie brigade emblem and the HumaniTeam logo, perfectly equal in size.

"Dad?" says Regina. "Where are we?"

Mr. Herrera finishes parking the car before he answers.

"What's going on, Dad?" she demands.

"Regina," he begins. "You trusted me, and I'm going to trust you in return. I thought you'd want to see what your mother and Chief Wachs were working on. They came up with a truly audacious idea—something you're going to *love*—"

"What about Nix?" says Regina.

"This solution doesn't require leaving all our lives up to such an unreliable individual . . ."

"Dad! We have to get him before Sky finds him."

Her father pauses.

Regina tenses. "Dad. What did you do?"

In the silence that follows, Regina's whole body goes rigid. She can tell by the set of her father's jaw, the way he won't meet her eye.

He's betrayed her.

"Nix is in good hands, honey," says Mr. Herrera. "It's all taken care of."

Shock and fury rush through her body, making her tremble. "You told Sky where to find him, didn't you?!"

Her father winces and stares straight ahead. But when he finally turns to her, his eyes are full of conviction.

"I'm really sorry, Regina," he says, sounding pained. "But please understand. My first priority is what's best for *you*. That takes precedence in this situation—and always."

"You have no idea what you're doing!" she shouts. "You've ruined *everything*."

Sky's thugs will extinguish Nix on sight to hide the existence of Project Phoenix. The zombies will rage and consume, and Sky will get everything he wants—more fighting, more violence, more death.

More reasons to make people depend on his superchillers and Cloudbusters.

"You have no idea what you've done," Regina says again, more weakly. The fight is draining out of her. It's too late. She has lost.

Humanity has lost.

Despair settles on Regina's shoulders like a heavy weight as she gets out of the car at her father's insistence. The air is thick with moisture—a terrible fog that closes them off from the world.

Her father ignores her powerless anger and leads her inside a tall and narrow building that looks a little like an air traffic control tower. They climb up to a room with a view over the airfield. It's full of computer monitors, and brigadiers and HumaniTechs working side by side. And at the center of all the activity, Regina sees her mother beside Chief Wachs.

"Hey, honey," says Dr. Herrera brightly.

Regina just glares at her mother. "Are you in on this, too?"

"In on what?" she asks, looking genuinely confused.

"We'll talk later, Celeste," says Regina's father.

Regina and her mother lock eyes for a moment, but then she turns away, back to her work. Regina feels a chill in her chest but has no choice other than to move forward, one foot in front of the other.

On the display screens, Regina recognizes at least eight different views of the town of Redwood—some showing the moonlit ruins, and some taken with a heat-sensitive infrared camera. On each, there are different views of the same story:

Redwood is like a half-made sandcastle, trampled before anyone ever got to see it complete. The zombies are consuming it with furious industry.

Chief Wachs speaks into a headset, amidst what sounds like a complex game of chess. "C5, D5, E5, give 'em a push. A7, A8, A9, drop 'em some bait."

After a chorus of confirmations, half the helicopters hovering above the town begin deploying powerful jolts of supercooled water from cannons mounted to the helicopter's belly to keep the zombies from spreading out in different directions, and the other half are dropping bundles of zombie bait to lure the horde onward. A path of bread crumbs . . .

"Keep 'em together," says Chief Wachs. She refers to her tablet, which shows a map of the town and beyond.

"Do you see what they're doing, Regina?" asks her father, attempting a smile. Like the argument is over, and now everything's normal again.

Regina turns away from him.

He continues his cheerful explanation. "Controlling the horde with a carrot and a stick. Moving them toward the sea. Your mother's plan is to lure both hordes of zombies together into the same place . . . To make them collide, and use the heat in one horde's veins and the cold in the other horde to extinguish each other."

Despite Regina's intense despair, she admits to herself that their plan is very clever. In a different world, she'd be impressed.

"So far, so good," Chief Wachs says as she deftly coaxes the untiring horde to choose the path forward that she wants them to take. The path toward the sea. "It's working."

"And what happens if it *doesn't* work, Chief?" Regina asks.

"In that case, we'll have a fleet of Cloudbusters on standby," says Chief Wachs.

"You're okay with that, Mom?" Regina asks, surprised.

"Chief Wachs is a professional," Dr. Herrera answers. "It'll work."

"I hope you're right," says Regina, with no option but to watch powerlessly.

Somewhere, right now, Sky Stone and his thugs are closing in on Nix, she knows. She takes out her phone to warn Oliver Wachs, but she can see her father keeping an eye on her.

She doesn't care if he's angry, though.

She turns around and leaves the room. Fast as she can, she calls Oliver. "Get out, now," she says into the phone, before he even says hello.

"They're here already, Regina," Oliver's voice comes through the phone. "They know exactly where Nix is. What *happened*?"

Regina tells him about her father's betrayal. About Sky Stone's security teams coming to hunt Nix down.

Oliver tells her he's racing to the library, trying to get Nix somewhere safe, and promises to call her back as soon as he can.

Regina calls Joule next, suddenly feeling very much alone.

27

MINA

Joule is in her bunk, unable to sleep, looking around at the other girls all fast asleep. She's wondering if they're even aware of the dead zone thousands of feet below when she's startled by her phone buzzing.

She's getting an incoming video chat from Regina.

"Regina?" she whispers, climbing down from her bed and tiptoeing past the other bunks.

The weak satellite connection the ship depends on for internet makes it impossible to read Regina's expression, but even before Regina speaks, Joule knows that something's wrong.

"What is it?" Joule asks, heading to find a private corner to take the call.

"I told my dad everything," says Regina. "Trusted him, like you said. But he betrayed me. For my own good, he says."

Joule sinks into a corner, right there in the hallway. She listens as Regina tells her about the double hordes facing California, and how Nix could've possibly stopped it. How he was actually coming over to their side, somehow—fighting for his humanity. But now it's all ruined. He'll be extinguished, and lives will be lost, and the surge will destroy more homes and farms and roads, and possibly the entire coastline.

"What was I supposed to do, Joule?" asks Regina. "I honestly don't think getting people to work together is even *possible*."

Joule struggles with what to tell Regina. "I'm sorry, Regina."

"I really wish you were here right now," Regina says.

Joule sits on the hard metal of the *Undercurrent*, in the middle of the ocean. "I'm here," she says. "Team Regina."

Regina smiles. "Team Regina is over, Joule."

"It's *not* over," Joule insists. "You can trust Oliver to get Nix to safety, okay? And you can trust me, too. Help is coming."

"You're in the middle of the ocean, Joule," says Regina.

"I'll figure it out," says Joule, meaning it from the bottom of her heart. "Don't give up."

As she ends the call, she looks up and freezes.

There's someone else in the corridor with her.

"Katrina?" says Joule.

"Hey."

"How much of that did you overhear?" Joule asks, worried.

"Um . . ." Katrina looks embarrassed. "Well, I heard enough that I really want to be part of Team Regina, too. If that's okay?"

"Better than okay." With relief, Joule feels a smile creep over her face. But just at that moment, there's a disturbance from the other end of the ship.

It's coming from the control center.

Even before Joule and Katrina enter the gallery, it's clear something is terribly wrong.

"Anton?" says Joule. "What happened?"

"I—I—" Anton stumbles. "I mean, I don't *really* know . . ."

There's panic everywhere she looks.

"I'm getting nothing from the ROV," Dr. Aldi reports from the control center below.

On every screen, static is all Joule can see.

"I've lost the DSV, too, Hugo," Dr. Aldi adds, looking at the instruments before him.

"You can't have *lost* them," says Professor Halyard. "Not *lost* lost."

"I'm not getting any telemetry, Hugo. We *lost* them. The *Fluke* at least."

"We have to recover it. Reel in the umbilical cable."

"I've tried, Hugo. It's caught on something down there. It won't move."

Halyard sags. "How did this happen?"

Dr. Aldi doesn't answer.

"Anyone?!" Halyard asks, looking around the room. "How did this *happen*? The submarine Pinkerton stole takes two people to launch, so I know that *someone* on this ship has information about what she was doing."

Joule's eyes scan the room, but it's not until she looks across the gallery and sees Anton's expression that something clicks.

"Anton?" Joule whispers. "What did you do?"

Anton begins shaking. "I—I . . ."

"You were her accomplice?" Joule says, her voice rising. It carries to the researchers below.

Professor Halyard gestures. "Mr. Zarkovsky, would you come down here?"

Swiftly, Anton is brought down into the control center. Face-to-face with an intensely focused Hugo Halyard.

"What happened, Anton?" he asks, examining Anton like he's a specimen under a microscope. Not unkindly, but clearly it sets Anton's animal brain to the question: *Fight or flight?*

"It's okay, Anton. I'm only concerned about safety now. That's what's important. Right?"

Anton tries to speak, but no words come out. Then he nods. Grasping something in his pocket that gives him the courage to keep going.

"Just tell us what happened, Anton," Professor Halyard says gently.

"I helped her launch the sub," he says, unable to look Halyard in the eye. "Three buttons. Red, amber, blue. That's all."

"What was she attempting to do down there?"

"She took something down with her," says Anton softly. His voice carries all across the silent room. "It's experimental. From HumaniTeam. A depth charge, she said. Like a zombie stun charge. A way to incapacitate a group of zombies, designed to be effective against hordes that are immune to water. Using electricity, I think. She was working for Sky, so you can ask him. I'm sure he'll explain how this happened. I'm sure he'll fix it."

As Anton says this, a nervous murmur fills the chamber as discussion of this revelation sparks everywhere. Anton continues to talk to Professor Halyard and Dr. Aldi, but Joule can't hear what Anton's whispering.

She does hear someone whispering *her* name, however.

Joule looks around, and sees it's Katrina who is urgently trying to get her attention. "Joule!" she whispers, so quietly. "What if it's just the cameras?"

Joule doesn't understand. "What's the cameras?"

"The *Fluke*—what if it's *not destroyed*? What if it just lost its cameras?"

At Katrina's quiet urging, Joule turns her gaze toward the monitors.

There's nothing but static on the large one. But if she looks down at the console where Dr. Aldi sits, peering closely, narrowing her eyes, she can see that there's still *one* gauge that's slowly ticking up and down. The depth gauge.

It's so basic, everyone else looked right past it.

The Fluke *is still sending back a signal*, she realizes. But then she shakes her head. "That could be nothing, Katrina," says Joule, not letting herself get her hopes up. The expedition is already ruined, either way. And she needs to find a way to help Regina somehow . . .

But she puts all that to the side as she remembers: If the *Fluke* is still sending a signal . . . what if *Mina* is still down there, too?

Joule suddenly feels her stomach drop all the way to the ocean floor.

She turns to Katrina and sees that she's already made this connection.

Joule imagines it. A tiny, curious octopus . . . trapped, alone, far from the sunlight. Just clinging to the *Fluke*—holding out hope that help will come, if she can make it a little longer.

Suddenly, the idea of giving up is unthinkable for Joule. Mina *must* be protected. Joule's entire mind and body are united in this purpose . . .

"You're right, Katrina. Mina needs our help."

She takes a breath, and hope fills her again.

It's hard to deal with it, for Joule. Holding that hope inside her after everything with her father—after everything in New York—after her best friend Lucy and the Santifer family . . .

But compared to *not* having hope?

This is far better, she knows. She pushes onward, letting her confidence in her purpose sit squarely in the core of her mind and body.

Hope is like breathing, Joule suddenly understands. You can stop doing it for a little while, just like you can choose to hold your breath. But it's not something that you can ever *truly* live without.

As long as there's breath, there's hope, she tells herself, vaguely remembering the words from somewhere else. But they're hers now, she decides. They fill her up and set her squarely on her feet.

"Let's go, Katrina. We don't have time to explain it to Aldi and Halyard. Time to move."

Katrina bobs her head firmly up and down.

"I'll distract them, you get to work," Katrina says as she and Joule make their way down and across the control center without anyone questioning why they're there.

While the adults are arguing, panicking, not listening, Joule and Katrina move boldly, taking over Dr. Aldi's computer station without hesitation:

Katrina acts as a lookout, while Joule considers the unfamiliar controls, which are one part computer, one part video game, and one part completely incomprehensible.

"Don't overcomplicate it," Joule tells herself, seizing the control stick that looks exactly like it belongs in a video game.

As she pushes it forward, which she thinks should be "up," she looks over at the monitor and sees that the depth gauge hasn't changed.

It'd help a lot to see what's down there. But she knows that's impossible. She's going to have to fly blind—or not at all.

Thinking of Mina, Joule keeps working. In her mind, she imagines the small motor struggling. She imagines it caught on a rock or—or something worse.

She trusts the *Fluke* to hold together, jogging the controls back and forth and back and forth, hoping to get any response from the sub . . .

She searches in vain for any scraps of information available to her on the monitor, but the depth gauge is really all there is left.

The depth gauge stays pinned where it is, on the ocean floor.

Which is when Dr. Aldi returns to his workstation to find it occupied and interrupts unhappily:

"Kids . . . what are you doing?"

Katrina's eyes widen. "We can explain—"

"No time to explain," Joule interrupts, then sees Dr. Aldi's expression and starts to explain. "Look. It's right there on the screen. The *Fluke* is still sending its depth to us. That means it's still not destroyed."

Dr. Aldi looks at what Joule's pointing out, checking the instruments.

Joule keeps pressing: "But since you think it's destroyed, what harm could it do to let us try? We can't mess up any worse than you all did."

Joule forgets about working the controls as she argues with him.

"I think . . . you two might possibly potentially theoretically not be entirely wrong to jump in here . . ." says Dr. Aldi. He looks up at Joule, and at the forgotten control stick. "Why'd you stop, kid? Keep it up."

Joule blinks, and gets back to work.

With a fresh determination, Joule and Katrina assist Dr. Aldi, who focuses on the incomprehensible part of the workstation, trying to make the engines work a little better.

"How do we know if any of this is actually doing *anything*?" Katrina asks.

"There's no way to know," says Dr. Aldi. "We just have to keep going, and hope those depth numbers start to change."

Katrina and Joule look at each other, beginning to worry.

There's nothing to do but just keep going. To make it real for themselves: Their work here is making a difference. It might even mean the difference between life and death for an innocent octopus who must be terrified.

For Joule, it's an incredibly strange feeling. Or: It's two feelings, maybe. Three feelings. All the feelings, colliding with one another—

Under the sea, reality is shaped by the decisions happening here.

Or maybe the fate of the *Fluke* is already decided.

And Mina might have been plucked off and devoured as they sit here, fiddling with controls that aren't doing anything.

If the *Fluke* doesn't survive, none of them will ever know what the truth underneath it all ever was.

In Joule's mind, she imagines a scene from the seafloor: zombies piled on top of the little vessel, holding it down. The ROV is rugged, designed to withstand the huge amounts of water pushing down on it at the bottom of the ocean—so much weight, it's resistant to their attacks . . . but it's not invincible.

And tucked into a crevice, Mina waits for the end . . . her terror more real than any pale joy left in the surface world.

Joule turns and looks to Katrina for a little optimism.

But it's actually Anton's eyes she catches.

And in Anton's eyes, she sees how much he believes in her, despite their argument. How much it matters to him that Joule is fighting—for Mina, for them all—

And the weariness in Joule's brain burns off like the fog.

She visualizes a different reality, on the ocean floor.

With clear eyes and a clear mind, Joule's quiet desperation is transformed. "Dr. Aldi?" says Joule. "I think we should shut the engines down."

Dr. Aldi frowns. "Joule, I don't think it's time to give up yet."

"No, sir," says Joule. "I think we should use all the *Fluke*'s power to pump out ballast. Fast as we can."

Dr. Aldi suddenly understands.

"Huh," says Dr. Aldi, coming back around to the controls and taking over. Joule eagerly relinquishes them. "Because maybe if we make the *Fluke* more buoyant, fast, it'll be way more powerful than the little engines are. Pop that pup out of whatever it's caught on. Why didn't I think of that?" he says, regarding Joule with a new respect.

Amidst his swift, practiced motions, Dr. Aldi explains what he's attempting to do. They have to get the robot to pump out the water it's been holding inside its ballast tanks and replace it with air. This makes it want to float—turning it almost into a balloon—forcing it upward, all the way to the surface.

Almost at once, the numbers on the depth gauge start to change.

A huge wave of relief fills the room as the tiny robot's telemetry comes in: The depth gauge reads shallower and shallower.

The *Fluke* climbs and climbs, and their heartbeats slowly settle.

And Dr. Aldi looks at Joule and Katrina.

"Good work, you two," he says.

They're nowhere near out of the woods, Joule knows.

But the world is different than it would've been without hope.

28

MANHUNT

Oliver sprints at top speed toward the library, where he left Nix and Kirby.

The HumaniTeam trucks appeared on campus just minutes ago, but already every building seems overrun with security teams. Oliver knows they're just doing their job—that they have no idea about Sky's hidden agenda and the enormous importance of the zombie Oliver is hiding in the library—but at the moment, their furious activity actually comforts him.

It means they haven't caught Nix yet.

Oliver ducks and weaves, keeping out of sight of the security team, moving toward the staff-only entrance to the library. Which is when Oliver suddenly realizes that Del's racing to keep up with him.

Del's really improved his Manhunt skills, it's clear.

"Oliver!" Del hisses. "Hey! Wait up."

"I can't stop now!" Oliver calls over his shoulder.

"Oliver! Come on."

"Don't worry about it. Go back to your new friends," Oliver says, panting. He can see the HumaniTeam security up ahead, heading toward the library. They're just minutes away from finding Nix and Kirby.

Del increases his pace to run alongside Oliver. "I'm staying, Ollie. You don't have to tell me anything you don't want to, but I'm not leaving you out here alone."

As they run, Oliver feels grateful that Del has chosen to stay. "Look, Del. I'm really sorry I didn't understand how it was going with your dad."

"You're sorry?" says Del, frowning.

"How could your best friend not have known about something like that? I just—"

"No. Ollie," Del says, pulling Oliver down into the shadow of the student center. He points out an approaching security team Oliver didn't see. "Look. You've got it all wrong. I'm not mad at you! *You're* the reason he's still *alive*. If you weren't so brave and determined, my dad wouldn't have had a chance."

"Then what's with not telling me?"

"I was useless in Redwood," says Del. "I was in the way. I was weak."

"You're not any of those things, Del. You're a good human being. Don't be so hard on yourself."

"This is why I didn't want you to know," says Del. "I'm *not* being hard enough on myself. That's the whole *problem*. I've gotta get tougher. I've gotta learn to fight, like you! I don't need to be pitied, Ollie—I need to be *pushed*."

From the bushes, there's a rustling. Both Oliver and Del spin, on guard for anything.

But when a frazzled-looking girl comes stumbling out, Oliver gives a cry of relief. "Kirby!"

She shushes him quickly. "Ollie, what *happened*? The whole campus is on lockdown."

"Regina's father told Sky where to find us," says Oliver. "Speaking of—where's Nix?"

Kirby's eyes move from Oliver to Del and back again. "I let him out," she says quietly.

"You *let him out*?! What the heck, Kirby!"

"I had to! It was that, or . . ."

Oliver lets out a long sigh. "You did the right thing. I'm sorry."

"Who is Nix?" Del asks.

"Del . . . you *really* want to know?" Oliver asks. "There's no un-hearing what's going on out here."

Del looks Oliver in the eye and nods.

"Tell him everything, Kirby," says Oliver. "I need to call Regina and let her know Nix is on the run."

"Ollie." Kirby's eyes flit sideways, toward the hedges. "He didn't actually *run*."

Oliver's eyes widen. *Oh.*

Kirby goes back into the hedges, and when she returns, she's not alone. Del freezes, his eyes comically wide at the sight of the zombie beside her.

"Kirby, stay back!" Del shouts, springing into action.

Oliver grabs Del's arm. "It's okay, this is what we wanted to tell you about. His name is Nix and he's not dangerous. At least, I don't think so. Kirby?"

While Kirby explains what's happening with Regina and Nix, Oliver calls Regina to come up with a new plan.

"Did you find him?" Regina's voice comes through the speakerphone way too loud.

Oliver turns the volume way, way down, and whispers into the phone, "We've got him, Regina. We're safe for right now. But we need to get out of here. Where do we go? What are we going to do?"

"Good question," says Regina. "How long can you hold out?"

"I don't know. We're kinda hidden, but if you could get here soon, that'd be really—that'd be really, really good."

"Okay," says Regina, regaining her usual confidence. "Ollie, I'll figure out something. Hold out for one more night, and I'll be there in the morning, with a plan."

"We can do that," says Del, warming to this unexpected rescue mission. "But we need to get moving. Those security guards are heading this way."

Oliver makes eye contact with Kirby, looking for her agreement. "Just to say the obvious: If we survive, our parents will kill us."

"I'm totally in," says Kirby. "Least we can do after Nix saved our lives last time."

"Wait, what now?" says Del.

As Kirby explains the way Nix saved the Wachs family—and Del's, too!—Oliver ends the call. "Stay in touch, okay—?"

"Wait!" Regina interrupts him. "Ollie, no. Don't hang up. We need to set a meeting place and time right now, and then you need to keep your phones off or they'll track your location."

"She's right, Ollie," says Del.

"All night, no exceptions!" Regina emphasizes.

"Where do we go?" Oliver asks.

"Can we sneak him into the dorm?" Kirby asks. "Up in the lounge behind this tiny door, there's a crawl space."

"Yeah, hide him in plain sight, kinda?" says Oliver.

Del frowns. "Guys. The dorm is a zomb shelter. That's the worst place to take him."

Kirby and Oliver exchange confused looks.

"You didn't know?" says Del.

"We've been . . . otherwise occupied," says Oliver.

"Well," says Del, "then it's a good thing I've been working on perfecting my Ollie Wachs impression, I guess."

Del removes a notebook from his back pocket. As soon as Del flips it open, Oliver is impressed. "Ooooh—preeeetty!" says Oliver in admiration.

It contains a very pretty map indeed. And between Oliver and Del, they quickly come up with a plan to stay off the grid, with two meeting spots set for the morning—a primary location for ten o'clock and a backup location for an hour later, just in case.

Through it all, Nix watches with an unreadable look in his eyes.

As the call ends and silence reigns, a soft moan emerges from the zombie's throat.

He looks like he needs to go into hibernation, or feed.

Silently, Kirby goes over to Nix and puts her shoulder under his arm to support his weight.

"Let's go, Nix," says Kirby. "We can make it one more night."

29

SURGE

Outside the command post in the decommissioned naval air station, Regina steps into an eerie, red-tinged fog.

It's like the world disappears. The sandy stretch of land almost appears to return to its natural swamp-like state. Pools of blood-colored vapor lying heavily over everything in sight. Buildings and trees emerging from the murk. Helicopters rising and descending like they're not quite real.

Her mother's mission to force the two hordes to annihilate each other continues, even as the zombies move closer and closer to the dense population of San Francisco.

For better or worse, Regina needs their plan with Nix to work.

"Because if we *lose* Nix, then there will be no way to stop future zombie waves other than more and more Cloudbusters," Regina explains to Joule on the phone.

"Trust me, I know," says Joule, and she tells Regina about the disastrous test of the weapon that led to the failure of the entire research mission. "We're returning to the port. At least Team Regina will be reunited."

"It doesn't matter anymore," Regina says wearily. "There's no way you'll ever make it here in time. It's up to me to fix this problem on my own somehow."

"You're not on your own," Joule answers. "I'm on my way to you right now. With a literal boatload of really smart recruits for Team Regina."

But before Regina can respond, there's an enormous hissing sound from the Cloudbuster rockets on the launchpad as a group of the rockets are primed for takeoff.

"Hold on, Joule, I'll call you back. I think I have another problem to deal with."

———

Inside the command post, Chief Wachs and Dr. Herrera's work is reaching its crucial moment. "Full blast, right now," says Chief Wachs. "M9, M8, we want to keep them from turning south."

From a camera view high over the California coast, Regina sees two different unnatural disasters on a collision course: One horde on land ravaging the towns and farms as it rages. One horde in the water, moving down the coast, and racing toward the city in an extraordinary, irresistible sweep.

Chief Wachs continues telling the helicopters to encourage the land horde with bait, and harass them with supercooled water. "M7, M6, give me a sustained push. Soak them."

They're following Chief Wachs's orders, but there's a problem brewing.

The hordes are turning to march parallel with each other. Moving as a team. Like a school of fish, like an army of ants.

They move south as one unit. One organism.

Like a giant amoeba, staying tightly grouped together. Like cells moving through a giant vein. This is no coincidence. This is a strategy. Intelligence at work.

There's only one thing Regina knows of that can produce this kind of zombie cooperation.

A zombie general.

For a moment, Regina thinks that it's Nix betraying her, but then she remembers his plea to stay. He's trying to do the right thing. He wouldn't do this. But that means there's another zombie like Nix out there, one who can command the others. Yet there's no way any of these adults are going to trust her if she speaks up . . . even if *she* was interested in trusting *them*.

Regina feels a chill go through her. Things are getting out of control, fast.

"You're losing them, Chief," says Regina's father unnecessarily.

Chief Wachs ignores him and gives further orders. "N6, O6, P6, Q6—lures to the *west*! Don't hold back. Whatever you got, use it now."

Regina knows that it isn't going to work. There's nothing that can stop these zombies now. Nothing but the Cloudbusters.

"Are those rockets fueled and ready, Celeste?" Chief Wachs asks Dr. Herrera, as if reading Regina's mind.

Dr. Herrera doesn't look happy, but she nods. "Yes, but—"

"We're gonna need 'em," says Chief Wachs. "Right now."

"You're only making it worse," Regina tells them. "You need to stop. *Please*."

Regina's father turns and looks back at her, but she ignores him.

"I don't want those zombies near any living people, Dr. Herrera," Chief

Wachs says. "That was our deal. The promise you made me . . . Wrecked farms is one thing, risking lives is another. Launch the Cloudbusters."

Thirty seconds later, the first Cloudbuster rocket is soaring into the morning air, headed north. More follow, and Regina watches a powerful hailstorm bloom, precisely over the top of the zombie horde. But then, as the storm clears, it reveals something unexpected.

Or at least, it's unexpected to everyone but Regina and her parents.

On the screen, everyone witnesses the fatal flaw of Project Cloudbuster: One horde has been extinguished . . . while the other has been made a hundred times worse.

Regina can only bear witness. The chill in her grows into a stomachache.

On the screen, the supercharged amphibious zombies move at great speed. But they're not stopping to consume. They're sprinting straight down the coast. Aiming right for the city, as if homing in on a target. As if there's something these zombies have got a particular taste for now.

"They're coming for the Cloudbusters," Regina whispers.

"We need to evacuate everything," says Chief Wachs, watching in horror.

"What do you mean?" says Dr. Herrera. "The whole city?"

"Yes. San Francisco, the East Bay, everything. Including this facility. So take your daughter and go."

"Go where?" Regina asks.

"I have *no* idea," says Chief Wachs. "High ground, wherever you can find it." Regina's parents exchange looks.

The Herreras aren't budging.

"What's your plan, Carrie?" says Dr. Herrera.

"I'll try to buy us more time by moving as many Cloudbusters inland as I can. That surge is going to turn into something unthinkable once it's supercharged again by these rockets. And there's nothing you can do."

"How are you planning to move them? You can maybe get two on a helicopter," says Mr. Herrera.

"You got a better idea?" asks Chief Wachs.

Regina thinks fast, looking at the video. Watching as a lonely, malfunctioning Cloudbuster that has crashed into the sea bobs in the waves. It should've sunk to the bottom, but it's buoyed on a sheet of ice created by supercooled carbon leaking from its core.

Dr. Herrera thinks faster. "What if we just launch them all?"

"That's a much more efficient way to get rid of the rockets," says Chief Wachs. "But as we just saw, they'll make the surge exponentially more powerful."

"We can reprogram them," Dr. Herrera answers. "Tell the rocket engine to fire but stop the actual Cloudbuster core from triggering."

"Just use the engines and *nothing* else," says Regina's dad. "Like a bottle rocket. Engines only."

"And we crash them in the middle of nowhere," says Regina's mom.

"Could that work?" Chief Wachs asks.

"It has to," says Regina's dad.

"We still need to evacuate the city immediately," says Chief Wachs. "We can't protect them anymore."

Through all of this discussion, Regina is bothered by an idea in the back of her head. A solution that's just out of her grasp . . .

Then, as she stares at the screen showing the satellite video, she sees something that makes her laugh out loud. A patch of white bobbing up and down in the waves. A sheet of water, frozen by the malfunctioning Cloudbuster.

"Mom, you were right," Regina says. "We can use the rockets like you were using zombie bait. Lure the zombies out to sea. And before they feed on the rockets, we set them off. Trigger them in the water."

"In the water?" says Dr. Herrera. "But that would just . . ."

Regina nods eagerly. "It'd make an iceberg!"

"That's brilliant, Regina," her mother says, comprehending.

"We've been trying to *extinguish* the zombies," says Regina. "But we don't have to extinguish them—we just have to trap them somehow. And where better than in an iceberg?"

Quickly, Regina's parents race through a flurry of preparations. They need a boat, for one thing, which the zombie brigade hurries to provide. And they need to coordinate moving all the Cloudbuster rockets onto the boat, as quickly as possible. Certainly before the zombies reach the city.

They work smoothly as a team, as Regina marvels. It's strange how, after everything, the Cloudbusters are actually the key to possibly saving the city. At least for today, that is. But humanity still needs another way to stop zombie season for good.

She needs to get back to Stuxville and save Nix.

30

HIBERNATION

"How'd you get him to eat last time, Ollie?"

"I just . . . he just did it when I brought him the bag."

"Nix? Can you hear me right now?"

Nix is restless.

A great emptiness sits heavy inside him. The weight is a signal to seek his hiding place under the ground—the earth his blanket, its chill dampness stiffening his muscles . . .

But Nix doesn't allow himself to go into hibernation. Not until he must.

In a distant corner of his mind, Nix still hears a trash bag crinkle, and a voice talking over him.

"Nix, do you remember me? I'm Kirby Wachs. From Redwood? You helped us. We're trying to help you. Me and Ollie—and Regina's coming, you remember her, right?"

Nix remembers Kirby.

It's the only good memory he has, among all the ones that loop and linger in his mind. One on top of the other . . .

He's glad to see she survived. It doesn't change all the horrible things that Nix has been part of. But the decision he made that day proves that there is a glimmer of choice before him.

This new path forward has been writing itself into existence.

It begins with remembering.

Over and over, again and again, the memories linger and loop.

But they're from a different perspective now.

Nix no longer sees the world through his own eyes in these memories.

Instead, he sees himself, through other eyes.

It fills him with fear and revulsion, every time.

In each memory, he wants to run, but he can't. There are ten sap-and-blood-blackened fingers holding him back. Pulling him into that nightmare face. That terrible, unhinged jaw. Those soulless orange irises. Teeth tear into him, swallow him.

"Nix, snap out of it. Please."

"Listen, there are people here. Looking for you. We need to move. Now."

"Can you hear me? I don't know what to do."

Unfortunately for Kirby, Nix's concerns are elsewhere. He's much more worried about the memories than any present danger.

Nix can no longer remember what "life" was once like. But something of his humanity remains, enduring long after the muscles and the mind became so thoroughly inhuman.

As energy, the joy and curiosity that were once held gently in Nix's heart still persist. In fact, not only does this part of him persist . . . it grows larger as each memory plays out.

"Look, I kept him from getting discovered all this time. Now it's your turn to do something."

"We'll have to just carry him. Come on."

In the back of Nix's mind, he feels someone moving him. There's an instinct to strike hard and fast—

"Ahh! Ow!"

"Ollie! Don't drop him."

"He just grabbed my leg!"

The memories stop Nix from doing anything else to Oliver.

The memories stop him from feeding at all.

The muscles and mind that belong to the zombie resist this, but the life force within has grown vast in the quiet moment of remembrance.

That's how he came to be locked in the basement of the HumaniTeam office, he remembers now. While the rest of the horde ate and ate to fuel their escape from the ruins of Redwood, Nix only sat in the sun.

The hunger rose, but he didn't act on it.

He couldn't.

What happened to him in Redwood was transforming him in a way he didn't really understand.

He's so full of others' memories—others' lives—that it's impossible for Nix to separate himself again from the others he carries with him. The spirits of living things that he has consumed are guiding his actions more and more.

But just then, a liquid is forced into his throat.

Suddenly, energy rushes through his veins again, as the zombie body absorbs this fuel.

"NIX!" He hears the voice calling him back.

His eyes open.

"Nix?" he hears again. "What's happening to him?"

But even if he answers to the name, whatever he is now, it's someone new.

A hand reaches out to Nix and touches him softly. A cool, pale human arm.

"Kirby." Nix says the name, and it's like a phone call connects.

A memory—*the* memory—surfaces in his mind.

There's an arm reaching in this memory. It's the same cool, pale human arm. Kirby's hand.

She clings tight to Nix and pulls him out of danger, as the car with her family in it keeps speeding, to outrun the Cloudbuster-mutated version of his kind. It's not a story that appears likely to have a happy ending, Nix can see. The family has no escape from the icy-cold grasp of what hunts them.

But guided by the life force within him, Nix decides to fight for their lives, sacrificing himself.

It was supposed to be the end for Nix.

But it was just the beginning.

The memory keeps coming again and again, like cool water rising from the ground.

31

THE GYRE

Anton stands on the deck at sunrise, watching Dr. Aldi and Professor Halyard supervise the retrieval of the *Fluke*. Joule and Katrina are there as well, but Anton has kept away from them.

Nobody blames Anton for what happened, but it still feels like he failed, somehow.

What if he'd suggested that Pinkerton should trust her crew members? Could he have prevented this disaster? Why had he simply accepted Sky's version of the story? How many other tragedies happened unnecessarily?

As he considers this, the water off the side of the ship froths and rises up into a dome, before sloshing off the back of the scarred hull of the *Fluke*.

"We should get a few more answers now," says Dr. Aldi as the ROV is hauled back into its cradle on the deck of the *Undercurrent* at a painfully slow pace.

From just what Anton can see, it's clear that the vessel's survival is a miracle. There are holes torn in the metal, and every instrument is shorn away. Dings and dents cover every inch of the surface, and a burning smell in the motor seems like it'll be in their nostrils for days afterward.

"Well, there's certainly a *possibility* that the damage I'm seeing here *could've* been caused by something like the technology Anton described," Dr. Aldi says to Professor Halyard, after a quick survey of the damage to the *Fluke*.

"Dr. Aldi?" Anton says. "Would it be helpful to *see* some of the technology that Lieutenant Pinkerton was testing, maybe? To help you understand what happened? If some sort of malfunction was why . . ." Anton trails off, not wanting to say out loud, . . . *why Vic Pinkerton is dead.*

"That'd be *very* helpful, Anton," says Halyard.

"Agreed," says Dr. Aldi. "But, Hugo—if the damage to the *Fluke* is because of electricity, it wouldn't explain why every single part of the ROV that's made of plastic has disappeared completely."

Anton hears Katrina let out a little gasp.

He turns to her, and so does Joule.

"Does that mean something to you, Katrina?"

Katrina doesn't speak. Shy, like always. "No, no, it's nothing."

Joule elbows her in the side. "Just say it, Katrina."

Still, Katrina looks uncertain.

"Hey," says Joule, leaning close to Katrina. She points to the damaged ROV as she whispers in Katrina's ear. "That thing was on the bottom of the ocean, and everyone was ready to give up on it—but you spoke up, and look at what happened."

Katrina leans close to Joule and whispers back. Anton can't hear what she's saying.

"Tell 'em," Joule says softly.

Katrina still resists. Joule frowns, eyes narrowing.

"*Tell* them," she repeats, bringing everyone's attention back to Katrina.

Katrina swallows hard and pushes through her fear. "It's just, um—it's just . . . I was wondering: Where's all the trash?"

"The trash?" says Dr. Aldi.

"Yeah. You know, in the water. The island made of trash that we came out here to study. The Great Pacific Garbage Patch."

"Well, it's not literally an *island*, Katrina," says Halyard. "It's really more of a *soup*."

Instantly, Anton gets that familiar patronizing feeling of adults-humoring-the-kids. But then Dr. Aldi and Professor Halyard both seem to feel the question reverberate inside them.

"Hey, Aldo?" says Halyard. "Where *is* all the trash? We're in the gyre, right?"

"We *are* in the gyre, Hugo," Dr. Aldi says. "It should be polluted. Plastic stew, gacking up everything."

"I've been so focused on the dead zone," says Halyard. "Could we be off course?"

"Not enough for the waters to look like *this*," says Dr. Aldi, gesturing to the clear blue ocean.

Anton turns in a circle, looking at the sea . . .

Katrina's right. Tons and tons of plastic trash should be surrounding them right now. Anton's seen pictures of the environmental nightmare—oceans clogged with every kind of plastic waste imaginable—but these waters around them are pristine. *Where'd all the garbage in the ocean go?*

"Zombie bait," says Anton, remembering what Joule told him at the beginning of the journey. "Trash is better than almost any other kind of zombie bait you can find."

The words resonate inside Anton's head.

"The zombies have consumed the Great Pacific Garbage Patch," says Professor Halyard, his voice full of wonder.

"Isn't that ironic," says Dr. Aldi. "Zombies *healing* something instead of destroying it."

"The world is far stranger than you ever imagine it might be," says Professor Halyard.

Joule rocks back on her heels, Anton notices. He catches her starting to very faintly smile and looks away, embarrassed.

Focus on playing your game, Anton, he hears in his head.

He takes out the deck of cards in his pocket, almost without realizing it.

Standing there, he fidgets with them, mentally ticking off the order—about the time he gets to the double fours, he hears Joule's voice: "What are those cards for, anyway?" she asks curiously.

"Huh?" he asks. "Cards?"

He tries to hide them, even though it's obviously pointless.

"You carry them everywhere. What's that about?" says Joule.

Part of Anton is a little happy that she's paying attention to what he's doing. But still he freezes up. "It's nothing," he says defensively.

Joule looks hurt. "Just curious. Sorry."

Anton can feel Alek's judgment in that moment, telling him that there's no way for a good thing to happen if he's so closed off and doesn't ever take any risks . . .

"Remember that story about my family's fishing boat?" says Anton, before he chickens out.

Joule nods.

"My cousin and I were in the middle of a stupid card game when it happened. We were together, like always. He was my best friend. *Only* friend, kinda. We ran away from the zombie, but it was so big. We were like ants to it. And right at the edge of the boat, as we were going to jump—"

He doesn't have the ability to say the words. But Joule nods like she understands.

"You didn't want to just let the game end."

Anton shrugs. "Something like that."

"Wow," says Joule.

"Yeah. So. Cards."

"Do you still feel him with you?"

Anton's eyebrows lift. "How'd you know that?"

"Same with my dad," she admits. Then she gestures toward the cards. "That game. Bet it's better with more than one player, huh?"

Anton shrugs. "The more players the better."

"Teach it to me?" she asks.

"What, now?"

"Unless you want to keep those cards in your pocket forever."

Anton clutches them tightly, realizing what she's asking him to do: continue the paused game that he and Alek began. Defensively, he considers telling her no.

But the game can't stay paused forever. He can feel a shift deep inside his chest, and his stomach twists.

"Yeah, okay," Anton says. He sits down on the deck and teaches Joule, with half a deck of cards, how to play slap. She's really good at it right away. It's not even annoying, though, Anton is surprised to discover. Winning isn't everything, he begins to understand, his focus changing . . .

Play your own game, Anton.

But then they have to call time-out again . . .

"Zarkovsky," says Professor Halyard. "You said something about showing me the dangerous contraption that Vic Pinkerton's been secretly keeping on my ship? Where I sleep, and where all my friends are?"

Anton picks up his stack of cards. "I'll be back," he tells Joule, heading off with Hugo Halyard.

As Anton walks away, Joule calls after him. "Anton! You forgot your cards."

"Keep 'em! We're not done playing yet," he calls back.

Joule smiles and pockets the cards as Anton disappears into a bank of fog that's rising off the water.

Her smile slips a little as she watches the peculiar fog drift over the deck of the boat. Something about the way it moves gives her a creeping sense of unease.

The way it pushes against the wind.

The way each wisp of fog seems to have a will of its own.

One touches Joule and tries to cling to her even as she moves away.

She feels silly, but as she ducks away, it clings to Dr. Aldi instead. The scientist shivers. His breath hangs in the air.

It sparks Joule's memory of her late-night conversation with Kai Stone on the deck. There was a wisp of fog just like that, drifting up off the water.

It's strange that he's not up here right now. "Has anybody seen Kai?" she asks.

When no one replies, Joule goes to search for him.

But her worries only grow with what she finds.

The trail starts with a slimy patch on the floor of one of the corridors that runs down the entire length of the ship. Joule discovered it by slipping on it and nearly sending herself flying through the air before she recovered her balance.

Then, before she can decide what the slime is, she hears an alarming sound. Soft whimpering, coming from the distance. Behind a door, it sounds like.

"Um, hello?" Joule calls out, down the hall.

There's no answer.

She follows the trail of slime and it leads her to a door that's marked MECHANICAL. Not a door Joule is familiar with. And when she tries the knob, it's locked.

When she rattles it, the whimpering grows louder.

"Hey!" Joule calls out. "Hello? Do you need help? Can you open the door?"

When nothing but whimpering reaches Joule, she tries to force her way into the electrical closet, but it's locked from the inside.

"Somebody help me!" Joule calls out, banging on the metal and making as much noise as she can.

She's about to run for help when she notices that the whimpering has stopped—

And from the crack under the door, *something* appears.

32

RACING TO THE RESCUE

Impenetrable fog covers San Francisco Bay as the sun creeps higher into the sky. Regina Herrera knows her father is out there right now, on a boat carrying dozens of Cloudbusters. The plan to lure the horde away from the city and imprison the zombies inside a frozen block of seawater is about to be put to the test.

It's both incredibly dangerous and the only chance they have.

When her father first volunteered to lead the mission, Regina resisted. Part of her worried he was only doing this to redeem himself in her eyes, to make up for having betrayed her. "Don't be a hero, Dad," she said, only half joking.

"Says the girl who's out here trying to save the world single-handedly."

"Oh, I've been using both hands, Dad." Regina held them up and grinned. It was the kind of corny joke that, in any sane world, should have made her dad laugh. But this isn't a sane world, after all, and her father only managed a weak smile. They both knew Regina's humor was an attempt to distract them from the truth neither of them wanted to acknowledge: that her father might not come back from this mission.

But if the worst happens, Regina won't be around to see it. She's heading back to Stuxville.

"Chief Wachs is going to take you," her father told her. "From what I hear, Sky's team hasn't yet caught your . . . your friend. I hope it's not too late to save him . . ."

"Thanks, Dad," said Regina.

And she hugged her father tightly, and then left before he could see her cry.

"Okay, Regina," says Chief Wachs as Regina climbs into the passenger seat of the car. "Spill it. What's happening in Stuxville?"

"I might've gotten Ollie in some trouble, Chief."

"Don't flatter yourself," says Chief Wachs with a thin smile. "My nephew is perfectly capable of making trouble for himself."

Regina smiles back, but it doesn't reach her eyes.

"Oh jeez, Regina. What *kind* of trouble are we talking about?"

Regina tells Chief Wachs everything. About who Nix is—and *what* Nix is—and how she needs to help him. How she needs to save Nix from an eternity in Sky Stone's horrible zombie research program, and convince him to send the remaining zombie hordes back to hibernation. To put an end to this devastating zombie season.

Chief Wachs falls quiet for a while before she finally speaks. "Nix. That's the name, huh?"

Regina nods.

"Okay," says Chief Wachs.

"Okay?"

"Your idea to stop the dead zone beat all of ours. If you have another plan I can help with, I will."

"You will?"

"I was across the battlefield from that horde in Redwood. I know there was something strange going on. An intelligence. And if you've found a way to reach him—to bring him over to our side?"

"I honestly don't know what he's capable of," says Regina. "Or what he's willing to do. But if I had to trust someone? I'd bet on a zombie like Nix over a person like Sky every time."

Chief Wachs thinks about this a long moment. "Okay, Regina. Buckle up."

They race toward Stuxville, accelerating wildly. As fast as Regina has ever seen a car go.

33

HAUNTING

"Please don't tell anyone I'm showing you this, Professor," says Anton, leading Halyard to the large crates that Pinkerton brought with her on board the *Undercurrent*. Crates that, now that she is gone, have for one small moment in time been left in Anton's care.

"It's a really important tool to fight the zombies, and I've been sworn to secrecy. If people know that HumaniTeam is working on it, it'll really slow things down at the worst possible time."

"Is that so? It might not be easy to hear, but a little bit of oversight might've saved your friend Vic's life, Anton."

Anton stands up very straight. "I didn't make the rules. If you don't like it, talk to Sky Stone."

"Sky."

"He's the one who asked me to do it. He's the one who has the entire world counting on him."

"He's certainly got the world *depending* on him," says Professor Halyard. "But that's not quite the same as *counting* on him. If there were any other choice than Sky Stone, I would prefer it, personally. And most of the people who know him best would agree, I expect."

Anton considers this as Halyard continues examining the contents of Pinkerton's crates. He gets the eerie feeling that Halyard is examining the contents of Anton's character at the same time.

"Professor?" says Anton. "Why are you working for HumaniTeam if you hate Sky so much?"

"I love it, Anton," says Halyard without hesitation. "Just how many deep-sea research partnerships with unlimited funding and total freedom to choose one's own missions do you think there are in the world?"

Professor Halyard takes the Eel out of its crate and looks at it with distaste.

"You came here at Sky Stone's personal request, correct? And the others—they found their way here like you, through the people in charge of this company. In my twenty years leading this project, a thousand kids like you have come with me on these expeditions." Halyard pauses. "None like *you*, of course, Anton. Or like Joule, or Katrina, or Kai."

Anton is surprised that the man knows their names. He's never spoken directly to any of the kids, as far as Anton knows. But then again, if you're studying something, you usually have to be careful not to influence it through your own interference . . .

"Are you *studying* us, Professor?" Anton asks. "Are you experimenting on us?"

Halyard seems taken by surprise by this, but he keeps looking at the Eel, now carefully loading it with a sticky-tipped electric shock bolt. A coil of light, strong cable is attached to the back—the cable draws blood where it pinches Halyard's finger. He grimaces, looking at the Eel like it's something toxic he just pulled out of the garbage patch that no longer exists.

"Even if most of this company is dedicated to building gadgets like this, the Halyard Project is really about building goodwill," says Halyard. "Sixteen kids a tour, three tours a year; we've built community here that knits us together. Connecting us to each other, and to our planet. Or that's what I've been telling myself, at least. We never really know if we're making any difference at all, I suppose."

Anton feels Halyard's sadness grow as he investigates the Eel more and more closely.

"You're making a difference, Professor," says Anton.

Anton tries to say more, but before he can do so, from the opposite end of the hall, someone screams for help.

Joule's heart beats fast and hard against her rib cage as a form takes shape before her. It's a zombie—that much is sure from the empty eyes and the wide, unhinged maw—but it's unlike any zombie Joule has ever seen or heard of. At first, it's like it's made of shadow. Of cobwebs. But as more and more of it oozes out of the gap under the door, it takes shape before her. Toothless, lips thick and swollen, eyes foggy white, with translucent, slimy skin, and bones right underneath. Bones that bend like plastic and spring back into shape again as it continues to rise up, gaining arms and legs.

This is where the garbage patch went, Joule's brain proclaims, despite the fact that Joule needs her full attention focused on dealing with the threat rising before her.

It's devoured so much plastic that it's turned into a new kind of zombie adaptation. One that is unlike any zombie I've ever heard of. It's more like a ghost, really, her brain carries on braining as the thing rises and rises, taller and taller.

Turns out that the old saying is true: You are what you eat!

The humor evaporates as the zombie tenses and leaps at Joule's face. The oily, slimy substance seems to coat her whole body—fiery cold pain erupting from her every nerve.

She tries to fight back but that just presses Joule and her attacker together more tightly as the zombie *feeds on her*—not using its teeth, but its very touch is like acid. Digesting her before she enters the creature's stomach.

The cry that starts in her chest as a terrified shriek dwindles to a nauseated heave by the time it emerges from her mouth, as the life in her blood is drawn out of her and into the monster, making it more and more solid, as Joule gets weaker and weaker.

She can't breathe. Her heart is beating too fast and not enough. But after all she's been through—

After everything she's survived—

Joule isn't giving in to that hopelessness again.

Suddenly, someone is tearing the creature off her.

"Joule?" says Guz Griffin.

Sudden relief floods into her as the more solidified zombie is slammed against the wall, hard. The zombie splatters against the wall like a mosquito against a windshield . . .

Griff shudders, not sure what just happened. He turns his focus to Joule's injuries. "Talk to me, Joule," he orders, no-nonsense.

But Joule can't talk quite yet. Her lungs are still heaving.

Which is why she can only watch as the zombie splattered on the wall begins to gathers itself back together.

"Hey, hey, you're okay," Griff says. He doesn't notice the ghoul . . . seeking, tasting the air.

Keeping her eyes locked on the almost spectral figure, Joule tries to warn Griff, but there's no breath in her lungs.

Accustomed to the lightless depths of the sea, it navigates by sound. By smell. By the air they exhale.

It lunges at Griff again, and Joule can do nothing.

But to her astonishment, at the far end of the hall, a voice calls out, "Griff, get back!" as Professor Halyard lifts a device that looks like a cross between a harpoon and a Taser.

A projectile slams into the zombie's chest and sticks there like glue. A cable stretches back from the sticky probe to the device in Halyard's hands, and the zombie stops in its tracks. Immobilized.

Joule can't bear to watch as the zombie loses control of its body. She turns away, focused on the locked mechanical closet.

"Door!" Joule croaks, pointing to the closet.

A soft moan comes from inside, and Griff attempts to open the door.

"Key? Key!" says Griff.

Halyard doesn't carry that sort of thing, though.

Griff looks around and sees nothing of use. But there on the ground, where it fell when he dropped it, is the metal mug Griff always uses.

With a swift motion, he snaps the handle off and shoves it into the crack of the door—

The entire door frame shifts and the door swings wide on its hinges.

Inside, there is a pale figure—

Kai Stone, who has been fed on like Joule was. Even more than Joule was.

"Kai?" says Joule. He's shivering badly. Shaking with fear and pain. She reaches toward him, and he leaps at her.

Joule can't even react before he wraps his arms around her chest and squeezes. It takes her a panicked moment to realize that it's not an attack— it's an embrace.

"Th-thank y-you," Kai whispers, teeth chattering, a thick sob in his throat.

After a moment, he releases her. He looks around at Halyard, Griff, and Anton.

"What happened here, Kai?" says Griff. "What are you doing locked in the mechanical closet?"

"I—I was trying to get away," says Kai. "Tried to hide, locked myself inside, but . . . but it came under the, under the—"

"Under the door," says Joule. "I saw it."

"Under the door?" asks Anton. "How did it do that? What *is* that thing?"

"It was like a ghost at first. But when we were trapped in there . . . the longer it fed, the more real it got."

"What do you mean it was like a ghost?" Professor Halyard asks.

Again, Kai struggles to speak. But Joule speaks up on his behalf:

"It was like fog, wasn't it?" Joule asks Kai.

In Joule's mind, she sees the fog wisps on deck—imagines them as undead beings, feeding on the crew. Slowly, at first . . . then too strong to stop.

"Professor Halyard?" says Joule, haunted by this. "I think we need to get away from here."

"I think you're right, Joule," says Professor Halyard. "We need to leave right away."

34

BEING

"Time to move, folks," says Oliver to Kirby and Del.

Hour by hour, step by step, they keep one move ahead of the HumaniTeam security forces that comb through every inch of Stuxville. It's much harder than eluding a zombie horde, but with Del and Oliver working side by side and brain to brain, they've managed it better and better as time goes on.

"Never thought our maps would be used for hiding a zombie being hunted by human beings," says Del.

"A zombie being," says Kirby, echoing Del with raised eyebrows.

Del didn't mean it the way Kirby heard it, it's clear—but sometimes we're the last ones to really appreciate something that we've long since known was true, deep in our hearts. And for Del, the idea that a zombie could exist on a spectrum somewhere between humanity and monstrosity . . . It's reawakening something in him—a curiosity and a joy that had gone missing.

"This way!" Oliver chooses a path, taking them back to the culvert where he and Nix sheltered two days earlier when they were sneaking into the Stuxville library.

Watching the sun rise higher into the sky, Oliver tries to guess at the time. Unfortunately, with their phones off so no one can track them, they really don't know how to tell when they're supposed to meet Regina. Not precisely enough. It might seem like a pretty silly problem to have, but it's also real. They just try to manage the best they can, and keep going.

And strangely for Oliver, despite the danger and the zombie who is tagging along, it feels like adventures used to feel.

It feels like being home.

Even if he's never going back there, he knows—not back to the way it was.

As Oliver feels the rhythm of his feet striking the ground—*beat, beat, beat*—balanced, confident, purposeful . . . it feels good.

The group makes it into their next hiding spot and everyone catches their breath—except for Nix, who looks like he's getting thinner and thinner with each passing moment.

Oliver takes out the green notebook in his pocket—still mostly empty, mostly forgotten—and on the page at the end he finds a passage faithfully copied over from his old notebook. *There's a difference between how to not die and how to live*, it says. And now he adds something new:

The way home isn't back, it's forward.

Despite how new the idea is to him, he feels totally sure of it. For all his love of Redwood, it's only a memory now. Maybe home isn't so much a place as a memory, he thinks. And maybe if we make as many memories as we can, our homes can become very large, and everywhere we walk, we'll remember the good that happened there . . .

But amidst Oliver's distraction, he hears a *snap* of a twig and suddenly pulls his thoughts back to his task. He looks around, searching for the source . . .

That's when Kirby screams.

Nix can sense a presence in the distance.

An incredibly powerful awareness. A *zombie* awareness.

Is this another zombie like me? Nix wonders.

But he has barely formed this question in his mind when he feels a heavy weight on his thoughts. Squeezing his consciousness. Pressing his thoughts down.

Without any warning, Nix discovers himself to be a passenger in his own mind. An extension of another creature—one much older than Nix. An ancient monster, newly awakened after a very, very long hibernation.

And in that immeasurable space of time, Nix's mind is perfectly clear.

It's the freest he's ever felt—free of hunger, free of rage, free of the need to keep going and going. While Nix's body is the puppet of a zombie that is much older than anything he imagined possible, Nix's mind is set *free*.

He feels all the good feelings that have been absent in his zombie existence. Old feelings, long forgotten. Curiosity and joy. Wonder and warmth. A breath of fresh air, heavy with promise of glorious discoveries, just beyond the curve of the horizon—

Then, as quickly as it started, it passes and he returns to his prison. It leaves him uncertain if it was even actually real. It leaves him longing for that brief taste of freedom.

But more than that, it leaves him deeply upset. Because before the ancient zombie presence released its hold on him, for whatever reason, she commanded him. This ancient, unnatural force has only one desire: to destroy civilization and make humanity extinct.

Nix has to warn them. Tell them to run—even if there's nowhere she can't reach.

———

As Kirby screams, Oliver rushes forward to free her.

"Hey! No!" Del shouts.

Nix is grabbing Kirby, Oliver realizes with a sudden panic. Everyone forgot for a moment that Nix is still a powerful force of destruction, unleashed and uncontrolled.

But Nix doesn't harm or feed.

"Nix!" says Oliver. "Let her go!"

By the time Oliver and Del pull Nix and Kirby apart, Oliver understands that Nix isn't attacking her; he is *defending* her. Putting himself between Kirby and a danger that Oliver hasn't even realized is there.

A human threat that Oliver turns to face—

A group of zombiefighters, arrayed around the opening of the culvert, taking the high ground. "Stop!" Del cries out, seeing one of them aim a superchiller right at Nix's chest.

Oliver, Kirby, Del, and Nix look out, realizing they're cornered.

"Outta the way, Del!" shouts a familiar voice as Del steps out in front, his back to Nix and his arms flung wide—

"Not a chance, Conrad!" says Del.

"Conrad?!" Oliver calls out, peering closer at the figures looming high above. They aren't HumaniTeam's security officers, he realizes. They're kids. All Del's Manhunt-playing friends, dressed in mismatched zombie-fighter gear.

Oliver looks from face to face, finally reaching Milo, and their eyes meet. "Wachs, what on Earth is going on?"

As Oliver considers how to explain—or even if he *should*—

There's a voice from behind him.

Raspy. Hoarse.

It's barely more than a moan. So soft that only Oliver hears it at first.

"Run," says Nix.

Oliver doesn't move. He stays beside Del, between Nix and Conrad's superchiller. He keeps his eyes shifting from face to face—

Nix repeats himself more clearly. "RUN," he says with all his strength, then repeats it over and over. "Run. Run. Run. Run."

Above them, Oliver hears gasps and surprised whispers. Oliver specifically notices Milo stiffening in surprise at the realization that the zombie is the one speaking . . . his cadaverous zombie vocal cords grating against each other. Milo's gaze travels from Kirby to Del to Oliver—and finally, to Nix.

"Wachs?" says Milo. "Start talking, fast!"

"He's on our side," says Oliver, acting much more confident than he really feels. "Please point your C-pack somewhere else."

"Move to the side, Del!" Conrad demands.

"Do *not* soak him, Conrad!" Oliver orders. "Milo, tell him to stop! You have no idea how serious this is."

Milo hesitates.

"I'm soaking him in three seconds!" Conrad warns.

"Stand down, Conrad," says Del.

Conrad just stares hateful daggers, not moving the nozzle at all. "Traitor," he says. And then he opens the nozzle wide.

"Conrad, no!" Milo bellows.

As a stream of supercooled water gushes out of Conrad's C-pack, Milo tackles him.

"Help!" Conrad shouts, trying to fight back against Milo. "Over here! Brigadiers! Anybody! They're brainwashed. I need backup!"

As Conrad and Milo battle it out, Oliver turns to Kirby and Del. "Let's get out of here."

Nix, Oliver discovers, has already started to flee.

His voice rasps as he retreats down the tunnel—

Nix's fear of the trickle of water running down the channel is outweighed by something else. By the words coming out of Nix's dreadful mouth, Oliver suspects it's not Conrad that Nix is worried about.

"She's coming." Nix's voice reaches Oliver, echoing off the tunnel walls.

"She's coming. She's coming. *Run.*"

In the distance, Oliver hears another sound.

A moan.

35

NO STONE UNTURNED

"Close call, Stone," Anton says to Kai as the *Undercurrent* moves at top speed away from the strange zombie and the dead zone it came from.

The wisps of fog can't move far on their own, and the same deep water and strong ocean currents that drew all the pollution in the ocean to the gyre will act as a natural zombie prison, according to Professor Halyard.

"Life's full of close calls," says Kai. "I for one am glad we came out here and tested that faulty weapon and discovered a brand-new bringer of the apocalypse. Fantastic idea."

Anton is pretty sure that Kai is being sarcastic, but he replies anyway. "Life's full of close calls, but not everyone gets a second chance, like you." Anton pauses, and feels a lump in his throat. "Like *us*, I mean . . ." he adds.

"Us?" says Kai.

Anton nods, his gaze drifting to the horizon as he thinks about Alek.

As he does, another voice joins the conversation.

"I'm glad we came, too," says Joule, approaching with a broad smile. She is carefully cradling a ballast tank from the *Fluke*.

"What's this?" says Anton.

As Joule reaches in, Anton sees a tentacle wrap itself around her forearm. She smiles even more broadly as seven other arms follow, and she lifts out a sea creature.

An octopus.

"Boys, I'd like you to meet my friend Mina," says Joule. "Do *not* be a jerk to her. Mina, this is Anton and Kai—they are also part of the team responsible for saving your life, so don't be a jerk to them." She looks from Anton to Kai. "I need your help."

Anton and Kai exchange worried looks.

"I need to get back to my friend Regina, who has taken it on herself to save the entire world."

"All by herself?" Anton asks, setting aside his past misgivings about Regina Herrera.

"Sounds like the Regina I know," says Kai.

Joule sighs. "Look, if you two aren't interested . . ."

Anton and Kai exchange a look once more. According to the ancient codes of such things, making eye contact twice in a conversation means you're friends now, like it or not.

"Good, then," says Joule. "And this is going to be a kind of ongoing thing, just so you're aware. Team Regina on three—one, two, three!"

Kai and Anton find themselves making eye contact an unprecedented third time as they follow Joule in exclaiming "Team Regina" awkwardly and with deep confusion.

"What do you think, Kai?" says Anton.

Kai shrugs. "Like you said. Not everyone gets a second chance."

Anton remembers Professor Halyard's comment about wishing he had someone other than Sky Stone to put his faith in. "You wanna learn a card game that has actual rules, Kai?"

Kai looks indignant. "I bet I already know it."

"Okay," says Anton competitively. "Show me what you got, hotshot."

36

ALL TOGETHER NOW

Regina holds on tight to the passenger door handle as Chief Wachs speeds along the empty highway and into the town of Stuxville. Regina feels a furious mix of hope and fear welling up inside her—she needs to meet up with Oliver and Nix and get to safety.

Nix is their greatest hope to make it through zombie season.

She's too close to lose him.

Too close to let anything get in her way.

But when they arrive at the place where Oliver told her to meet him, there's no one around.

Something's gone wrong with the carefully planned meeting Regina and Oliver set up. The road is empty, and so is the culvert underneath.

"Ollie told you he'd be here?" asks Chief Wachs, inspecting the area.

What if Sky found them first? Regina worries.

No, she thinks with relief. *If Sky found them, Oliver would've called for help.*

"They're on the run," says Chief Wachs, looking at the evidence on the ground, including signs of some kind of struggle. "Stay here. I'm going to follow the tracks."

"Hold on, Chief," says Regina. "I know where they're going."

Regina tells Chief Wachs about the backup meeting location she and Oliver decided on.

Chief Wachs pulls out her phone and consults some application called Mapmaker Alpha. "Is this the spot?" asks Chief Wachs, pointing to a location on a very detailed map. It looks like Oliver's handiwork to Regina.

"That's it," Regina confirms.

"Okay, buckle up," Chief Wachs says.

Chief Wachs isn't using the road this time, Regina soon learns. She's going right through the campus—moving among the buildings and HumaniTeam security checkpoints with unnerving speed.

They soon make it to the backup location where Regina and Oliver agreed to meet.

"There!" Regina says, spotting movement. "Is that . . . ?"

It's them. Regina recognizes Oliver in the distance, racing toward the meeting spot.

"Ollie!" Regina calls out. "Over here!"

Oliver hears her voice as he's racing through the campus—following the quickest, safest path that only he can find. He pours on even more speed, urging Del, Kirby, and Nix to hurry as well.

Chief Wachs presses the gas and races to meet them.

Nix is lagging badly behind. Forcing the others to slow down and help him. And behind Nix, there is what looks very much like a zombie horde . . .

But it's *not* a horde. It's a group of regular humans, chasing Oliver,

Nix, and the others. Some are ZDP kids, it looks like. And others wear the stealthy black of HumaniTeam security.

"Come on, Nix!" Regina calls out.

"They're not going to make it," says Chief Wachs, revving the engine and racing toward Oliver's group. She turns on her sirens as she drives across the grassy space.

But it's not enough. Nix is still moving too slow. The zombie is certain to be overtaken by the angry mob of humans—an irony that is not lost on Regina, even amidst the terrible situation.

Inevitably, from the crowd, one figure separates, and at last catches up to Nix.

Nix has no strength to resist. He collapses in the clutches of his pursuer.

"No!" Regina roars with fury.

The human who caught Nix doesn't tackle him to the ground, however.

To Regina's surprise, the human wedges his shoulder under Nix's armpit and *helps him*. Regina watches this, almost not believing her eyes.

When Chief Wachs skids to a stop to let everyone climb in, Regina jumps out of the car without realizing it. Instinctively, she races to help Nix as well, putting her shoulder under his other arm and helping him across the final distance to Chief Wachs's car.

"Inside, everybody!" says Oliver.

All the pursuers back off as Chief Wachs uses her siren to halt the crowd. None of them are willing to attack a brigadier in her cruiser.

In a huge pileup, Regina finds herself squeezed in beside Oliver, Kirby, Del, Nix, and the kid who chose to help carry Nix instead of extinguishing him.

"Hey, thanks for the help," he says. "I'm Milo."

"I didn't think you were on our side there at first," says Regina.

Milo just shrugs. "Everybody's full of surprises today."

The whoop of the siren pulls their attention back to Chief Wachs, who addresses the mob using her loudspeaker. "This zombie is in brigade custody," she announces from inside her locked car. "Everyone go back to your zomb shelter. Now."

After she repeats herself, the HumaniTeam security force begins to slowly, reluctantly retreat. But then something makes the officers pause.

A familiar sound reaches Regina's ears.

A helicopter, rotors chopping.

Even before she sees the HumaniTeam logo on it, she has a very strong suspicion that it's Sky Stone, racing to capture Nix.

"We have to get out of here," Regina tells Chief Wachs.

But it's too late to run now. Emboldened by their leader's arrival, the corporate zombiefighters have begun turning around. Encircling Chief Wachs's car once again. Not approaching yet, but not allowing them to leave.

The helicopter touches down on the grass nearby, and Sky Stone smiles and makes his way toward Chief Wachs.

"Stay in the car," the chief tells the kids tangled up in her back seat as she opens her door and stands to face the arrayed forces of HumaniTeam.

"I need the zombie back, Chief," says Sky.

"I'm not giving you anything while you're threatening my nine-year-old niece," says Chief Wachs.

"That zombie is part of a crucial HumaniTeam research project," says Sky.

"Research," says the Chief.

Regina sticks her head out the car window. "Would you like to explain to the entire class what sort of *research* you've been doing, Sky?"

Sky ignores Regina's question and continues to address Chief Wachs. "Turn the zombie over, Chief."

"Or what?"

"You want to find out?" says Sky, dangerously quiet. "For starters, I'll make sure that California loses their Cloudbuster supply. There are plenty of places across the world that would *love* to have a way to protect their communities. And if that doesn't work, we'll see how you do without superchillers, too."

As Sky blusters on about the punishments he will level if Chief Wachs doesn't turn over Nix, he's stopped short when his breath catches in his throat. A sudden, hot gust of wind arrives, carrying with it the smell of rotten eggs . . .

It's choking. Unbreathable. Even with just a window cracked open.

There is a flashpoint forming nearby.

"She's sending a horde," Nix rasps with a haunted, faraway tone.

"Who?" asks Oliver. "What do you know?"

Nix blinks and shakes his head, as if to clear a fog from it. "Run, run now."

"Hold on," says Kirby.

As Nix struggles, Kirby reaches into her pocket and produces a sleeve of peanut butter cookies. She shoves them, plastic and all, down Nix's throat. And he doesn't look happy about it. He looks quite disturbed, in fact.

But his eyes brighten a little. And his voice comes more easily . . .

"She's like me, but . . . she's—she's—she's very old. And she's very strong. Still awakening. Run—*now*."

It's impossible to run, though. All escape routes are cut off by HumaniTeam security officers.

Nix isn't done speaking. "Regina!" he says, his voice rough but stronger. "She is taking control of us all. Telling us—"

Nix's eyes go wide with shock.

He's fighting something, it's clear.

Something that's in his head.

He begins to moan. An awful, pained, agonized sound.

"Nix?" says Oliver.

"She wants us to feed on humans," Nix says. "Just humans."

Regina and Oliver exchange a look. So do Del and Milo. Kirby just holds Nix's clawlike hand, comforting him the best she can.

Kirby reaches into her backpack, pulling out another sleeve of cookies.

"Hold on, I have one more pack."

"Don't!" says Nix sharply. "Don't—feed—me."

"You need fuel," says Kirby stubbornly.

Nix just shakes his head. "Please. I—"

His eyes widen again. But this time, Nix is prepared. He stays in control.

"We need your help, Nix," says Regina. "You have to fight back. Take control of the others."

Nix looks at Regina—wanting to do as she asks. But he hesitates.

And in that split second of silence, distant moans come from the dark. Everywhere. Every direction.

"Please, Nix," says Regina.

As the HumaniTeam security officers ringing the cruiser hear this as well, they find themselves caught between intimidating Chief Wachs . . . or turning to face the unknown darkness, and all its unknown dangers.

"Regina?" says Oliver. "Nix is going to help, right? After everything we did to help him?"

Regina locks eyes with Nix. "Yes, he's going to help," she says.

Nix wants to say no, it's clear to Regina. He wants to lie down and rest.

After everything she did to help him.

There's a prickling on the back of her neck, and she can *feel* the horde closing in on them.

Another betrayal.

Fury fills her, and intense heat.

"Stay with us, Nix," says Regina. It's the command he gave her once. And she is determined to command him now. Regina feels a connection between herself and Nix return. A searing heat and a stomach-churning chill.

Regina keeps her eyes fixed on the half human, half zombie before her.

For a moment, Nix looks totally surprised. Unprepared.

Compelled to obey her command.

Understanding comes first in a trickle, then in a rush. There's a line Regina has just crossed. A line that's hard to take back. *No, no, I didn't mean it like that*, she tries to say. But the words won't come out.

Nix's eyes harden. The humanity in them grows more distant, and the flat, terrible orange grows stronger. That vulnerable human half of him has lost control, and in its place is the monster once more.

Meanwhile, Regina feels like she's plunged into an icy cold river. Like it's about to carry her away, pulling her under. There's no way to breathe. Her mind narrows and narrows until she can't hold on to a thought. It's a nightmare.

The zombie horde breaks through the earth. All around the car, orange eyes flare brightly, and the heat of their bodies is almost overwhelming.

Fury and greed.

Hunger and rage.

With a rising terror, she feels the unquenchable need of the horde all around them.

Eventually, though, Regina feels herself become strangely comfortable in the furnace-like dome of hot air. And then she feels her ability to think returning, without the shocking chill eating into her.

Which is when she realizes that she shouldn't be comfortable. Something's not right.

With a sinking horror, Regina realizes the hunger that drives the horde is inside herself, too.

She's in the horde, with Nix by her side.

The zombie horde is overwhelming the humans defending their home.

And Regina, to her extraordinary surprise, is on the wrong side.

She's among the zombies, and they see her as one of their own.

Their commander.

37

LANDFALL

In the shoaling waters where the Pacific Ocean meets the San Francisco Bay, the surge first appears like giant jellyfish floating in the water. These are the crowns of the giant zombies' heads, emerging from the sea. Stringy hair matted, milky irises roving. Their open mouths gargling seawater and anything that's in it . . . including a giant cruise ship loaded with people trying to evacuate, but much too late.

For the passengers, the outcome is inevitable. The horde leaves little more than a splinter of wood behind as they move on, their hunger only more intense.

As the zombies' torsos rise from the sea, the grotesque figures hardly have anything human-looking left about their features. Bloated, with a bioluminescent glow, they seem to have much more in common with the creatures native to the sunless depths of the ocean than whoever they once were long ago.

They move closer to the panicked city where the citizens of San Francisco are now frantically seeking higher ground. Racing in every direction, clogging every form of transportation. Every road and bridge—

As they do, there's a second, much faster vessel motoring down the channel toward the surging giants.

At the front of the vessel is Regina's father. Speeding through the bay and toward the sea, Mr. Herrera catches the attention of the engorged, lumbering zombies.

One after the other, they stretch out their fingers toward the boat, like sharks in a frenzy.

The boat escapes somehow, only to slow down and wait for the zombies to pursue . . .

Again, it darts close to the zombies, and again, it draws more attention.

It's *daring* the zombies to give chase. Luring them away from the populated city, using the Cloudbusters they seek so intently as bait.

With each taunt, the zombies grow more enraged and fixated on the ship.

The reason for their enthusiasm is clear if one can see the cylindrical objects on the deck:

Forty-eight Cloudbuster rockets, all lined up side by side.

Or: forty-seven, actually . . . One of the cylinders has fallen over and rolled to the very edge of the deck. As the vessel banks to avoid a zombie's giant hands, it finally tips off the side and falls—

Almost before the rocket touches the water, it is immediately devoured. A moment later, the zombie that ate it grows even bigger. It swells into a colossus . . . rising up into the sky like some bizarre zombie Statue of Liberty.

"Catch me if you can, big guy!" Mr. Herrera roars.

As Regina's father weaves and maneuvers, the Cloudbuster rockets tumble around the deck, loose now after all the sudden jolting. But there's nothing he can do about that. Mr. Herrera has to focus on making sure to stay close enough to the zombies to keep them completely focused on the Cloudbusters and lead them away from the city.

Gradually, he works them farther and farther into deep water out at sea. Away from the population of the city, he races on, eluding the clutches of the zombie horde.

That's when the boat shudders and screeches.

They finally caught him, he knows.

They're all around, suddenly.

He's surrounded.

That's okay, though.

Mr. Herrera always understood it was unlikely he'd make it back from this mission. At the very least, he's kept these zombies occupied long enough to buy the people of San Francisco time to evacuate and get inland to higher ground, where the surge can't reach.

Regina will be okay, he thinks to himself as the zombies tear chunks out of the hull and the Cloudbusters roll chaotically across the deck.

As he watches, the Cloudbusters slam into the rail and topple overboard into the sea.

And then there's a phenomenal underwater *boom*.

"There! I can see it!"

From the deck of the *Undercurrent*, Joule spots the San Francisco skyline etched into the horizon, just for a moment as the morning fog finally lifts. The ship has made top speed, trying to reach the city, but the supersurge has clearly already arrived.

In the water off the coast, there is a battle going on between the amphibious zombies and a ship of some sort.

Or . . . at least, that's the assumption Joule makes from a distance.

By her side, Anton nudges Joule. "Something's wrong up there," he says.

"Yeah," says Joule, and calls out, "Professor Halyard?!"

"I'm aware, Joule!" Hugo Halyard calls back to her.

It's not until they close the distance a little more that she can squint enough to see that the battle is oddly . . . paused. Stuck in a moment of time. There are dozens of giant zombies attacking a helpless, capsizing ship—but it's all encased in ice.

Joule might have had trouble believing her eyes, except by this point the entire crew of the *Undercurrent* is on the deck of the ship, watching the unsettling sight of colossal zombies unable to move inside the newly formed iceberg.

"What could've *done* this?" Joule asks.

It must've been instantaneous.

They were flash frozen somehow.

"It reminds me of home," says Anton. "Only, back there, it was giant zombies coming *out* of glaciers as they melted."

"Zombies coming *out* of glaciers?" Joule repeats. "But how could there be zombies trapped in ice that's been there for thousands of years . . . ?"

Anton shrugs. "I didn't stop to ask questions," he says. Then he looks frustrated. "Maybe I should've, though."

Joule turns to give Anton an encouraging smile. But as she does, she's distracted by something on the zombieberg below.

"Hey," says Joule, "is there someone moving down there?"

"Is there?" Anton cranes his head to look.

There's a man on the capsized ship, waving at them. "Help!" Anton calls out. "Man overboard!"

Joule stiffens in surprise as she keeps looking at this survivor in disbelief—

"Mr. Herrera?!" Joule calls out.

38.

Oliver Wachs is shaken to his core. "Regina?" he calls out. "What are you doing?"

He can only watch as she and Nix race out of the car, without warning.

"Where are they going?" asks Kirby.

"Is this part of the plan?!" asks Del.

Something isn't right, it's clear, by the intensity of Nix's orange eyes. An orange reflected in Regina's eyes as well.

Oliver looks to Kirby, and he can tell before she moves that she's about to chase after them.

"Don't," Oliver says.

Oliver's sister ignores him and runs.

"Kirby!" he calls out, sprinting after her.

But neither Kirby nor Oliver makes it very far. Sky Stone's security team moves to stop them, and there's no way to evade this. "Nix!" Kirby cries out when she can't go any farther. "What are you *doing*?"

Nix and Regina are inside the horde, Oliver sees. Are they trying to control it?

"Nix!" Kirby calls out again. "It's time to rest, like you wanted! You need to tell them—tell them to *rest!*"

Amidst the zombie horde, Nix seems to notice Kirby. He can hear her, see her.

It's hard to tell if he can understand her, though.

"Everyone back to the zomb shelter!" calls out Chief Wachs, grabbing Oliver's wrist.

There's a temporary truce between Sky Stone and Oliver's aunt, he sees. They're joining forces to prepare for a battle with the undead. Superchillers at the ready. The zombies seem to keep appearing without warning.

"I'm calling in a Cloudbuster launch," says Sky.

"There are no Cloudbusters *left* to launch," says Chief Wachs, explaining how they are currently being used to keep the dead zone attacking San Francisco at bay. "Or at sea, more accurately," Chief Wachs adds with a nervous laugh.

The zombies and the HumaniTeam security forces are locked in a fierce battle, back and forth, as Chief Wachs manages an improvised retreat to the safety of the zomb shelter. From the back seat of his aunt's car, armored against zombie attack, Oliver navigates with his map, helping the brigadiers stay a half step ahead of the zombies threatening to overwhelm them.

Oliver and Kirby make it inside and find their mother anxiously awaiting them—simultaneously relieved and furious. But the prospect of being grounded for life doesn't carry all that much terror for Oliver, given how short a time the rest of his life might actually be. From the upper floors of the dorm, HumaniTeam security officers and Chief Wachs fight side by side to defend against growing waves of undead that seem to be interested in only one thing: hunting down humans.

The zombies ignore everything else.

It's chilling to behold.

It's impossible to look away.

Oliver is completely unprepared for this. These zombies are breaking all the rules about how the undead are supposed to behave. And yet, it feels inevitable to Oliver at the same time. If there's one thing that unites all the zombie lore from the time before Oliver was born, it's that zombies' lethal hunger is focused on the living versions of their own kind.

But Oliver suddenly thinks back to when they were together on that hilltop overlooking Redwood. He was freezing cold, he remembers . . . and then, a moment later, Regina had somehow warmed him, as if there were a furnace in her chest. He'd blocked it out . . . but now he remembers it all in a brand new light.

Oliver can't help but try to make sense of what he saw happen to Nix and Regina in his aunt's car. Nix seemed to lose control of himself, the monster taking charge. And Regina seemed to give in to something very similar, too. To a monster within herself.

Oliver considers this and wonders: If a zombie could be half human, then why can't a human be half zombie?

What if instead of helping Nix escape his worst instincts, Regina somehow pushed him back down that monstrous path, and unexpectedly got pulled along after him?

Oliver looks across the crowded rooftop where so many of the other people who've been sheltering here have gathered to watch the roiling bodies, rather than stay in their beds and imagine it.

Oliver is packed in tight beside his parents and Kirby and Del. All the ZDP kids are there, too. And even Sky Stone, who isn't a zombiefighter. Oliver looks around at the others on the roof with a nervous worry.

What if that's how we'll all end up one day? What if turning into a world-destroying monster is just part of being a person?

Why does it only happen to humans?

Unthinkably, as Oliver wracks his brain for answers to these terrible questions, he finds himself plunged into sleep. It's too much for his brain to handle, and it just shuts down. And the next thing he knows, he's been carried to his own bed, and hours have passed.

He can still hear the fighting outside as day turns to night. He imagines the sun setting over a sea of undead, on all sides.

They can't get inside the zomb shelter . . . *yet*. But through the dark hours, it constantly seems like they're going to come rushing up the stairwell and explode into view at any moment.

And in a half-dreaming, half-waking state, Oliver endures nightmares that don't distinguish dreaming from reality.

Wherever Oliver is, he can see a terrible face out of the corner of his eye.

An old face. The face of the powerful, ancient zombie who Nix warned of, Oliver instantly knows.

He has a hard time focusing on her features. When he tries to focus on her eyes, all he can think of are grasshoppers. When he tries to look at her face, all he can think of is the shell of a walnut.

It's like she's not really there. Like his brain is trying to make sense of shadows cast on a wall. Of something unimaginable.

And even though it's impossible for Oliver to stand up to her, in Oliver's dream, there is someone who *does*.

A boy Oliver's age, who looks a little like Nix, but with eyes that are still human. "Stop," says the boy, almost silently.

Below, the zombies pound and pound on the strong doors of the zomb shelter, trying to get inside more than ever. And the pounding is the shadow's voice.

"Stop," the boy repeats.

The zombies pound and pound, not obeying.

The boy closes his human eyes, and when he opens them again, Oliver can only see little volcanoes of tiny red ants.

Stop. The word is less a sound than the absence of it.

Like a lullaby.

Like a warm blanket over his exhausted body.

It's a very great surprise to Oliver to awaken an instant later, and discover that the horde of zombies no longer pounds and pounds at the doors of the zomb shelter.

There's stillness in the world once again.

Oliver goes to the window, and the sky is just bright enough to make the campus visible.

And with the dawn, Oliver witnesses Nix and Regina stumbling back to the zomb shelter, each supporting the other.

Two halves braced against each other, to guard against falling down.

As they stumble forward, the zombiefighters order them to stop, super-chillers at the ready, nozzles aimed.

And then another figure races in between them—

Along with Regina's mother and father, Joule arrives on the campus of Stuxville University just in time to see Sky Stone's zombiefighters preparing to soak Nix and Regina, and she doesn't hesitate to sprint and get in the middle of the situation.

"Back off!" cries Joule.

Regina's mother and father are only a half step behind, and they instantly get the HumaniTeam security forces to stand down.

Oliver leaves the window and sprints downstairs. He doesn't care that his parents are shouting for him to stay—there's no way he can get in any *more* trouble than he already is. Which is just beginning to sink in, since it's seeming increasingly likely he's going to survive this. But that's future Oliver's problem.

Right now, Oliver focuses on slipping through the zombiefighters and making it to Regina's side.

Regina looks like she's been through torture.

Her body is covered in bruises and soot. Her eyes are wild and full of fear.

Oliver barely notices Nix being roughly tied up and taken away under Sky Stone's stealthy supervision.

Oliver is totally focused on Joule and Regina. He watches as Joule quietly pleads for Regina to stop fighting. That she's okay. That she's sorry she didn't get here in time.

Finally, Regina seems to realize where she is. That she's surrounded by people she knows. People who care about her. Uneasily, he watches as Regina's eyes go from Joule to Oliver to her parents, to—

She looks around, searching for someone.

Her mouth works, but there's no sound right away.

"Nix?" Regina croaks. "Where's—?"

"You need to rest, Regina." Joule tries to settle Regina down.

Far in the distance, the helicopter with the HumaniTeam logo is disappearing off into the sky.

"Sky?! Did they take Nix? We have to—!"

"He's gone, Regina," Joule tells her gently.

"We have to stop him!" Regina demands.

Oliver and Joule look at each other.

"Sky Stone is going to put Nix in the deepest, darkest, most secure zombie research lab he can find," Regina says, her eyes full of both determination and desperation.

"We're not going to abandon him," says Oliver.

"But we're not going to let you take it on by yourself, either," says Joule. "Whatever we do, we do it together."

"A rescue mission?" says Regina uncertainly.

"Yes," Joule says. "And we'll need a boatload of the bravest, smartest, most stubbornly optimistic people in the world to pull it off."

Regina looks at Joule with raised eyebrows. "You think your friends would really do that? Drop everything to save a zombie?"

"After people hear what just happened here, Regina? I won't be able to *stop* them."

Oliver catches Regina and Joule looking at each other, united. Strengthening each other. Then they both turn to look at Oliver.

"What do you think, Ollie?" asks Regina. "You want to go get Nix, and try to save the world?"

For the first time, Oliver doesn't have any question in his mind about whether he belongs.

"Let's get started," he says.

OLIVER, REGINA, JOULE, AND ANTON HELPED AVERT A CATASTROPHIC
ZOMBIE SURGE, BUT THE BATTLE HAS ONLY JUST BEGUN. NIX HAS A
DANGEROUS SECRET—ONE THAT'LL CHANGE EVERYTHING THE KIDS
KNOW ABOUT THE ZOMBIES . . . AND WHERE THEIR LOYALTIES BELONG.

DON'T MISS THE EXPLOSIVE NEXT INSTALLMENT!

ZOMBiE SEASON

BOOK 3

THE BATTLE HAS BEGUN.
DO YOU HAVE WHAT IT TAKES
TO JOIN THE FIGHT?

Regina, Oliver, and their friends need YOUR help figuring out how to defeat the zombies. Meet up with Regina at her top secret base where you'll be able to:

Fight zombies and collect supplies.

Read confidential files and uncover dangerous secrets.

Share theories with other readers.

And much more!

SCAN THE CODE TO GET STARTED, OR VISIT SCHOLASTIC.COM/ZOMBIESEASON FOR MORE INFORMATION.

ABOUT THE AUTHOR

JUSTIN WEINBERGER is the author of *Reformed* and has contributed to numerous television dramas, including the FX on Hulu series *The Patient* and FX's *The Americans*. Justin lives in Brooklyn with his wife, Chelsea, and their dog, Penny.